TERESA
OF THE NEW WORLD

TERESA
OF THE NEW WORLD

SHARMAN APT RUSSELL

YUCCA

Yucca Publishing books may be purchased in bulk at special discounts for sales promotion, corporate gifts, fund-raising, or educational purposes. Special editions can also be created to specifications. For details, contact the Special Sales Department, Yucca Publishing, 307 West 36th Street, 11th Floor, New York, NY 10018 or yucca@skyhorsepublishing.com.

Yucca Publishing is an imprint of Skyhorse Publishing, Inc.®, a Delaware corporation.

Visit our website at www.yuccapub.com.

10 9 8 7 6 5 4 3 2 1

Library of Congress Cataloging-in-Publication Data is available on file.

Cover design by Yucca Publishing

Print ISBN: 978-1-63158-042-0
Ebook ISBN: 978-1-63158-052-9

Printed in the United States of America

To my father

PROLOGUE

In 1528, Spanish ships landed near what is now Tampa Bay, Florida. Three hundred men and forty horses marched inland to explore the New World. Eight years later, the remaining four survivors of that expedition met up with Spanish slavers in northern Mexico. One of these four, the renowned Álvar Núñez Cabeza de Vaca, would eventually write and publish a report of his adventures for the King of Spain—the true-life story of a *conquistador* who became a trader for the coastal tribes of Texas, then a slave of those tribes, then a shaman, then a conquistador again.

This story, however, is about the girl who never appeared in that report to the King of Spain—a girl who could listen to plants and stone and deer. This story is one of those hidden things, rising from the earth and kept hidden in the earth. This is a story remembered by a few, reimagined, remade, returned. In this story, animals and people know each other. Words are alive, and power runs through our veins, through everything, everyone, like water rushing to sea, each day bringing its own amazement.

1

Later, Teresa remembered.

When she was a child, the earth whispered to her as she lay on her stomach, her stomach pressed to the earth. Often this happened when she was hungry, and she was hungry often, for her people lived in a difficult, swampy area along a mosquito-filled bay where they ate fish and roots and not much else.

One day she woke to find her cheek pushed hard into prickly grass. She didn't know how she had gotten here. The last memory she had was of her mother nursing the new baby. Although Teresa had lived four winters she had just recently stopped nursing, when the new baby came, and that had been sad—for her mother to feed someone else and not her. She must have left her mother then and fallen to the ground and gone to sleep. Now she felt dazed, her stomach empty, a distant ache. The earth beneath her also felt distant, far away and cold. Her naked body was cold. She wished someone would cover her with an animal skin.

In a hollow voice, her empty stomach complained to the earth. Her stomach told the earth she was about to die of hunger. Her stomach said it was glad because it was tired of being so empty and unhappy.

The earth rippled with a kind of amusement. Teresa listened, a skill she had learned because of her father. No, the earth said, she is not going to die. She is only a little hungry. She should eat some dirt now, mixed with water. She should look around for some roots or grubs.

She can't, her stomach complained. She can't move.

The amusement in the earth swelled. Go find some leaves, the earth whispered. A grasshopper, an animal skin to chew.

The ground under Teresa seemed warmer, and Teresa tried to burrow into that warmth. I love you, the earth whispered, not to her stomach but to her throat and mouth. I love humans. I love watching you. I love watching and wondering what you will do next.

Her stomach grumbled. Teresa spoke out loud, "Tell me a story."

The earth said, I will tell you about a girl with long black hair who could swim through rivers of stone. She moved through stone as wind moves through the branches of a tree. Once she followed a vein of fire to a lake of fire, and she swam there smiling at all the bright fish, yellow and orange and red and blue. She had never seen anything so beautiful, and when she swam back up and rested on the ground, as you are resting here now, she held one of those glowing fish in her hand. Of course, it burned her. She dropped the fish with a scream, and the fish fell on the grass and burned the grass and died. She was sorry then, with her hand on fire. She is not from your tribe. She lives in the mountains.

Teresa didn't much like this story, which had ended badly for the girl. What are mountains? Teresa asked drowsily.

Oh, I love mountains, the earth said with a thrill that prickled across Teresa's skin. Sometimes I rise into the sky until I am high above myself looking down on myself, and I can see so much and so far and the mystery of what I am is almost clear to me . . .

"Teresa!" Someone else was speaking, a human voice. "Teresa!" Not very gently, her father shook her arm. "Wake up! Eat this." Something in Teresa's mouth felt too big against her tongue, and slowly she began to chew. A baked prickly pear pad. He must have gotten this from her aunt, who Teresa had seen gathering prickly pear that morning.

"Come," her father said. "The men are fishing on the shore. Let's build a fire and watch them."

Her father was not a good fisherman. He was not a good hunter of rabbits or peccary or a trapper of mice. He did not seem to know what plants to gather or how to prepare them. In truth, he rarely found his own food. Yet he ate as well as anyone and usually had something to give to Teresa. All this was because her father was a good trader, taking seashells and oyster knives from her tribe to the tribes inland and bringing back deer tassels dyed red and a special paste for making arrows. Her father could do this because he was a stranger and no one's enemy and because the tribes in this area considered him lucky. They thought themselves lucky to have such an interesting creature live among them, a man so absurdly incompetent, with a ridiculous long nose, blue eyes, and hair flowing down his face and chest. They were not sure if this creature was human—not even Teresa's mother was entirely sure—but they treated him with kindness and gave him food.

"They are a generous people," Teresa's father told her more than once, and she agreed. Her people were generous. They fed new babies, and they fed her father.

Years ago, her father had come to this bay of salty water, shipwrecked in a small barge with other men like him. One by one, the other men died or left until her father was, as he often said, "Alone in the wilderness! Like Christ, Our Lord!"

It was her father who had named her Teresa and who spoke to her in the Spanish of Seville in southern Spain where he had been born. It was her father who told the best stories, wrapping her in his arms and language, whispering about a life she did not understand, although understanding seemed to form just beyond the swampy bay, waiting there for her to grow older. Kings. Cloth. Books. Writing desks. Teresa delighted in the images that distracted her from the mosquitoes or hunger in her stomach. Even when the story confused her, she caught certain words or phrases, ideas like fish, bold and surprising, tasting of her father's mind. She had learned quickly to nod at her father then and speak back to him in the Spanish of Seville because he needed her to do this, because his need surrounded her like the sea and sand.

"*Buenas tardes, Papá*," she could say by the time she walked on uncertain legs. Only a few months later, she spoke in sentences. "Yes, Father, it is so hot!"

Dramatically then, her father would stretch out his arms and lift his face to the hazy white sky. "Thank you, Heavenly Father, for giving me this young child, this comfort in my exile in a heathen land. With all my poor bleeding heart, I praise Your name. Yea, although I have been abandoned and forsaken, still I praise You!"

More often than not, this kind of performance made Teresa laugh. "You are my queen!" Her father would grab her under the shoulders and swing her through the air until they were both dizzy. "My precious queen!"

"Tell me a story," Teresa would beg when she could breathe again.

And often—as he did now, as they watched the men fishing with spears and nets—her father told her *the story*, how he had left his home in Spain in the year 1527 as the Royal Treasurer of the Pánfilo de Narváez expedition, how he had come to be shipwrecked here in this mosquito-filled bay to live with Teresa's grandfather and mother and aunts and uncles.

There had been prophecies. Before the ships sailed, a woman warned the Spanish crew that they would never leave the New World. Or rather, most would never leave. But God would work miracles, extravagant miracles, for the few who did.

There had been magic. On the island of Santo Domingo, in a storm that killed sixty men, her father had heard silver flutes and bells. The howling wind stopped his breath and thumped his head like a furious parent, yet the wind also held the sound of tambourines. "And this was strange," her father said, "not the usual instrument of angels."

Later, when they landed in *La Florida*—named for Easter, the season of flowers—the men marched away from their ships and began to die from disease and hunger, from the arrows of the powerful Apalachee. Desperate, the Spanish killed their horses and used the flesh to make leather thongs and water bottles. They built barges to sail west along the unknown shoreline. Lost at sea, more of them died of thirst, and some went mad and jumped into the water to drown.

That was when their leader abandoned them. Her father still spoke bitterly of his captain, Pánfilo de Narváez, that greedy man who took the best boat and rowers and disappeared over the horizon, shouting, "Save yourself! I cannot help you!"

Finally, in another storm, a huge wave took her father's barge and threw it onto the sandy shore*, juego de herradura,* as far as a horseshoe can be tossed. On this beach, years ago, Teresa's tribe had come to feed the strangers. Her people had brought fish and fresh water, and the Spanish had given them glass beads and copper bells. "Your mother helped carry wood to the beach," her father said. "We were naked and cold and would have died without that fire. Even then, half-dead, even then I marveled."

Teresa struggled out of her father's arms and ran not far from the smoking fire they had built of green wood. Almost immediately, the mosquitoes found her. She urinated and brushed at the insects. Her mother said the winds were coming soon to blow the pests away. In the night, too, there would be some relief. Quickly, Teresa returned to the smoke and her father's body, where she fitted against the curve of his chest.

"Go on," she commanded. Next he would tell her about the men who stayed with her people only a short while before they walked west into the setting sun, seeking Spanish outposts in New Spain. Her father had been too sick to go with them. Soon Teresa's relatives had also become sick, and some of them died. They defecated dirty water. Their skin burned. They shook as though the Bad Spirit were shaking them from the inside. Many people in the tribe had blamed the Spanish and wanted to strangle her father, but her grandfather argued against it.

Teresa hummed a song she had made up about mosquitoes being carried off by the wind. She leaned into her father's hairy chest, and he grunted. Recently he had allowed his wife's brother to pierce one of his nipples and insert in the hole a reed two palms long and one finger thick. The wound was still tender.

"Then I was born," Teresa said with satisfaction. "After you went to eat blackberries with my mother."

"You are the daughter of a nobleman," her father murmured. "My paternal grandfather was Pedro de Vera, the conqueror of the Grand Canary."

"But I am not noble," Teresa reminded him, for she knew this part, too.

"No, you are a bastard," her father said as he stroked her hair.

She was full of blackberries and lay relaxed on her back on the ground, her stomach rising up nicely rounded. Her mother and aunts picked nearby, half the berries in a woven basket, half into their juice-smeared mouths. Directly above Teresa, the narrow leaves of a tree began to move, rustling and jumping like one of the little dogs they kept for food who played on the beach running back and forth barking at a wave. The wind was the wave. The rustling leaves were the excited little dog.

Under Teresa, the earth whispered that it had a secret. Do you want to know my secret? the earth asked. Of course, yes, Teresa answered. Then you have to tell me a secret of your own, the earth whispered. Tell me what you dream about at night. Tell me why you like blackberries. Tell me the name of your baby sister.

That's more than one secret, Teresa pointed out, but she smiled as she said this. None of these things was really a secret. This was just a game the earth liked to play.

Tell me the secret your grandfather tells about *me*, the earth demanded.

The soft ground seemed to shift and flow around Teresa, and she molded her body to fit the movement. She began the story, which also was not a secret: my grandfather says you are a large turtle walking through the sky. You move your arms and legs slowly, and you travel beside your sister, another turtle, who is also walking through the sky. You go so slowly and so carefully that all the tribes can stay on your back like the babies of an opossum.

I am traveling through the sky? the earth asked, pleased.

And we travel with you, Teresa said.

"Ter-e-sa!" Again a human voice interrupted their conversation. This time, the voice belonged to Teresa's mother, bending down and close. Her mother's eyes were brown, highlighted with gold around each iris. Her berry-smeared lips curved up, for she was almost always happy. Now she was happy at Teresa so full of blackberries. "Ter-e-sa," she repeated, sounding as she often did a little confused by the foreign name. It was not one she could pronounce easily. "Run to your father and take him to your uncle's house. Your aunt says there is something for him there."

She spoke in the language of their tribe, and Teresa answered back in the same language. "Where is my father?"

"In his bed, of course!" Her mother showed her white teeth. The new baby hung on her chest in a sling of rabbit fur, a piece of wood strapped to the back of the baby's head. A flat head would let everyone know to whom this child belonged. Opening her eyes, the baby began to cry. Automatically, Teresa's mother put a nipple into the tiny mouth.

"But first, let me squeeze you," Teresa's mother bent closer to her older daughter. "Oh, you smell good. Come back quickly and you can help us."

This didn't sound so wonderful to Teresa.

"I'll teach you a song," her mother promised.

As predicted, her father was sleeping in his hut on a bed of crushed oyster shells. From the walls of the house, Teresa took a straw and poked his callused feet, so that he jerked to throw the insect off. "Pest!" he said in Spanish when he saw her. She straddled his stomach and sat down. Inside the round house, the dark air was cool. A small door let in the sun that slanted on her father's legs. The rest of his body was hidden in shadow.

"My mother wants you at my uncle's house."

"She has a knife to trade."

"You are going away!" Teresa realized with surprise that she had not realized this before. When people started giving things to her father, it meant he would be leaving the tribe soon.

Her father jiggled her on his ribs and sang a song about a mule—an animal, he explained, like a horse. Fiercely he tickled her rounded stomach so that she had to laugh, although the movement combined with so many blackberries was making her sick. Finally he stopped and cupped his rough hands around her face. "Ask your mother to comb your hair," he ordered.

"I will," Teresa said to please him. She didn't think her mother had time to comb hair. This was the time to gather berries, and the women worked all day long.

"Take me with you, Papá. I'm ready now."

"You are a baby. You would still drink from your mother if you could."

"Take my mother, too."

"Like the Italians with their feuds and labyrinthine strategies for war, your people are enemies of the inland tribes." Her father spoke now in a deep ringing voice that Teresa loved. "Your mother would be killed," he said sonorously. "But I am a trader and a curiosity, belonging to no one and not a slave. As a stranger, I am fed and welcomed."

"Take me with you," Teresa entreated again in Spanish in the cool dark house of grass. Her father shut his eyes. He seemed close to tears.

"When you talk to me and I close my eyes," he said, "I could be home and you are running toward me, my little daughter dressed in your finest clothes, begging your Papá to take you to a fiesta."

Pobrecito, pobrecito! Teresa thought. Her poor father missed his home in Spain so much! He missed his Charles the Fifth so much! Teresa pretended to feel sad.

"The Capoques are also a generous people," her father murmured to himself and to her. Later she would remember every word—she, the blank page on which he wrote. "The Mariames sometimes kill their female children at birth. The tribes inland can be cruel but often have great love for each other. It is noteworthy that these people take only one wife, except for medicine men, who may have more."

Teresa played with the long gray hairs on her father's chest. The wound around the reed had closed over, and she hoped the charm would bring him fortune as her uncle had promised. More hair grew from his chin and cheeks, although he tried to keep his beard trimmed with an oyster knife. The hair on his head was also gray, mixed with red and brown, an extraordinary color.

"Giddy-up," her father crooned, his eyes still closed. "Imagine yourself, Teresa, on a beautiful horse, a horse you would have if you were a boy and not a girl, a beautiful bay mare."

Teresa bounced cheerfully. "Papá, Papá, Papá," she chanted. "Take me with you."

Her father left the tribe early the next morning. In the dark round house, he picked Teresa up from the crushed oyster shell bed. "Wrap your legs around my waist," he whispered, and she did, clinging to him in front while his rabbit skin pack dangled behind. Beside them, her mother stirred. Her father told his wife to sleep. Hmm, hmmm, Teresa's mother sighed, and the baby sighed, too.

Teresa didn't ask why her father had changed his mind. She didn't think to say good-bye to her mother or sister or grandparents or aunts and uncles, also sleeping in grass houses nearby. A silver mist shrouded the northern hills, the colors of the earth gray and silver, the white water in the bay barely emerging from a pale sky.

"I must tell you something, Teresa," her father spoke seriously. "You must understand that this is no ordinary trading trip. By now, on my travels, I have heard of more survivors from the Pánfilo de Narváez expedition, good men all, who sailed away in the other barges. They live as slaves with the coastal tribes to the south, and they are treated very badly by these people. My own good friends, the ones who left me to walk to Mexico City—those men are all dead, captured and killed by these same bad tribes. Now I know for certain no ship is coming."

Her father paused for breath. He walked slowly, burdened as he was with her and all his goods for trading. Behind them, Teresa saw a peccary emerge from the scrub brush. The animal stood as high as her waist, its body covered with coarse black and white hair, its flat nostrils wet and twitching. Something reached out to Teresa, and she heard the peccary say . . . what? The animal was speaking to her. But the images—pictures like words—wavered, unclear. She didn't understand.

"What?" she said out loud.

"Someone," her father was saying, "has to walk west again."

He murmured a Spanish song, a sailor's song, as he carried Teresa into the gray breaking light. She could feel the good fortune burning in his chest, in the reed two palms long and one finger thick. She could feel the excitement running through her veins, and she could see crackles of magic shoot from her father's body into clumps of prickly pear, saltbush, and locust trees. She gripped her father's waist tightly with her legs. He was the one for whom God would work miracles. He was the one who would walk back to Spain, all the way home.

2

Teresa remembered walking beside her father, his steps too big so that she had to hurry, always hurry to keep up. When she felt tired, he sang songs to distract her, and he told stories, the story of their own adventure as they traded north and west while he hunted rumors about poor shipwrecked men like himself. Finally he decided they should go south and bargain with the coastal tribe that held one of these men—a Christian named Andrés Dorantes.

Unfortunately, instead of letting Dorantes go, the tribe enslaved her father as well. Teresa saw with surprise how easily they grabbed and threw the trader to the ground, how they even took his goods of paste and deer tassels. Now like Dorantes, Cabeza de Vaca was beaten and mocked, made to carry loads of firewood and dig pits for baking cactus. He no longer sang and barely spoke to Teresa.

On her part, she was treated well by a foster mother who gave her food, boiled roots or the occasional bone and meat from a rabbit or deer. Gently, the foster mother combed Teresa's hair and cuddled her during the cold nights. She praised Teresa, saying that someday she would be a powerful woman.

"I can hear the peccary," Teresa boasted. "I can hear the earth speak."

"You are special," the woman agreed lovingly.

14

This foster mother watched and soothed Teresa the day she was tattooed, four blue lines under each eye, four cuts rubbed with ash, making her a member of this tribe. Now Teresa could marry one of the chief's sons. Now she was valuable as a female who was not a relative and not someone who had to be bought from another group. "Now you are my daughter," the woman said. "My only child."

In the summer, these people went to gather prickly pear in a large field of that cactus, where they were joined by other tribes who all came together peacefully. Everyone was happy to eat so much red ripe fruit. Everyone put aside their grudges—at least for a time—and danced and drank day and night from clay jars of juice they had buried in the ground to ferment. Teresa also danced and drank and watched as her father and Dorantes slipped away to meet with another Christian called Alonso del Castillo and the black Moor Esteban, both slaves in other tribes, both from the Spanish ships. Suddenly her father seemed alert and gay again, quickly doing whatever he was told to do, secretly meeting with his former comrades whenever he had the chance.

One night, once again, he came for her, this time before dawn, motioning for Teresa to be quiet and taking her from the side of her foster mother, who slept heavily under the glittering stars. Again he lifted her up in his arms.

At the appointed place outside the cactus fields, the other men protested.

"You can't bring a child with you," the Moor Esteban said. His skin seemed to blend into the night, and his hair curled like the wool on a buffalo.

"They will follow her," Andrés Dorantes exclaimed. "They will want her back."

But her father insisted. "We will be careful. We won't leave any trail. She comes with me."

"This is your daughter?" The third man, Alonso del Castillo, spoke as though he couldn't believe such a thing. He was taller than Teresa's father, with bulging eyes like a frog. "How old is she?"

"Five years," her father said proudly.

"But she is a heathen!"

"No, listen, Alonso." Her father nudged Teresa. "Say your catechism."

"We don't have time for this," Dorantes hissed.

Without effort, knowing the words perfectly, Teresa recited, "*In nomine Patris, Filii et Spiritus Sancti. Famulis tuis Domine subveni, quos pretioso sanguine redemisti. In nomine Patris. Redemisti! Redemisti!*"

The three men stared at her.

"Now sing in Spanish," her father commanded.

Teresa thought of all the songs she had been taught, comedy from the minstrels in the marketplace, love songs and homesick songs, songs of longing for the country of Seville. "*Río de Sevilla,*" she began obediently, "*de barco lleno, ha pasado el alma, no pasa el cuerpo . . .*"

"Enough," her father said.

"We should go." The Moor seemed resigned. "I know of another tribe far enough away who are not friends with any of the groups here. I know their language a little. We are four men. Perhaps they will see us differently if we have a child. We won't look like warriors."

Teresa let her father take her hand. This time, she knew what was happening. This time, she knew she would never see her foster mother again. Her foster mother would wake up reaching for her daughter. Her foster mother would shout and run through camp weeping. Teresa's sorrow swelled in her throat. She couldn't breathe or talk. She let her father take her hand and pull her forward.

They traveled to the next tribe, where they were given some roots and asked to heal a sick woman who complained of headaches. Her father shrugged and made the sign of the Cross over the woman's head. Immediately, the woman jumped to her feet declaring herself cured! Now other men and women came forward to be cured, and her father made the sign of the Cross over them, too. These people also jumped up, perfectly well, and each gave her father a handful of dried fruit.

Teresa was impressed by this gift, and so were the three Christians and the Moor, who decided to stay awhile with these friendly and generous people. Although they meant to move on after they had rested, winter came suddenly, and it was a bad season, bitter cold with hardly any rain. No one had the energy to travel now. And soon no one had anything left to share. That was Teresa's sixth winter, and she was hungry in a way she had never been hungry before. Now when her stomach spoke to the earth, the earth whispered back: well, yes, if you are *too* empty, *too* unhappy, then you will die. I will still love you. I will still be with you.

Should I die then? Teresa asked the earth.

Wait, the earth suggested, a few more days. A few more days, and then a few more days, and it will be spring, and you will have green shoots and grasshoppers and baby mice to eat. Don't be in a hurry.

Soon after that, the Moor came and gave Teresa a bit of dried peccary meat, and she did not die. After that again, they moved to another group of people, who ate the mesquite beans that hung from a thin-leafed tree, the raw beans tasting sweet and crunchy, the dried beans ground into flour that could be carried in a leather bag. In a summer full of mesquite bean gruel and mesquite bean paste, they traveled from group to group, Teresa walking beside her father, always walking toward the setting sun.

Everywhere they went, they healed people of headaches and illness. Her father was the best healer, with his eloquent voice and face raised to the Heavenly Father. But Andrés

Dorantes also cured stomach ache and the disease that made people sleepy, and so did the Moor Esteban. Only the third Christian, frog-eyed Alonso del Castillo, held himself aloof and looked sour whenever his companions made the sign of the Cross.

"Sacrilege!" he sometimes whispered out loud. "Imagine— if the priests knew!"

"Look around you," Dorantes would sneer back, "and tell me what you see. Do you see any priests?"

In one tribe, Teresa watched her father cut into a man's chest with a flint knife. Months ago, an arrowhead had lodged near the heart and a scar grown over the injury, which still pained the man and made him weak. Her father reopened the skin so that blood ran into the hollow made by the ribcage. When her father cut deeper and drew the arrowhead out, bright blood flew up and dotted her father's brown and red beard mixed with gray, his long nose, and his thin lips. He blinked and shook his head. Quickly he used a bone needle and fox hair to draw together the lips of the wound.

The man watched her father calmly, as though this were happening to someone else. He lay on a grass mat and looked up into her father's eyes, which shone like bits of blue sky. Teresa shivered when she saw that the air around these men no longer moved as air moves, flowing and shifting. Instead it held perfectly still, while the energy in her father's body and in the man's body rose up like another skin above their skins, hovering in a layer of glowing heat that dove suddenly back into the sick man's heart.

The man reached for her father's hand. Her father smiled and covered the fingers with his own. "You will be fine now," he spoke in Spanish. "You will feel no pain. You will be well. You will rise up from this bed tomorrow. The Lord will bless you and keep you as a symbol of His Mercy and His gifts to us."

Now the man's wife took the arrowhead and showed it to her relatives in the village, and the next morning the man did rise from his bed just as Teresa's father had said he would, and this healing ran ahead of their journey so that they heard about it at each new place. Each time, the story was a little more extravagant until finally people said the healer could raise the very dead from the ground.

This upset Alonso del Castillo more than usual.

"What is wrong, Alonso?" her father asked, winking at Teresa, who sat under a nearby mesquite bush.

"I will not be part of this blasphemy," the other man's voice rose as he paced back and forth. "We are not righteous. We cannot heal the sick or make the lame walk or raise the dead! I am a sinner, like you, like Dorantes, even like the Moor. I have done things in this country . . . There are things I don't want to talk about."

Teresa's father stood and grabbed his friend by the shoulders. "God has given us this grace and mercy, Alonso. When I bless and cure each man, each woman, I pray to Our Lord, and so does Dorantes. Each healing brings us closer to home. This is God's will! Everywhere now, the tribes welcome us."

Alonso del Castillo began to cry, the tears leaking from his eyes and running down his cheeks spotted with sores and inflammations. "You see this as a way to get to Spain. I see this as a test of my immortal soul."

As if moved by these words, suddenly gentle, her father comforted the Christian, and they cried together and then prayed, sobbed, and prayed again. Teresa sat under the shade of the mesquite tree, saying nothing but thinking that Alonso del Castillo's bulging eyes looked about to pop from his face, his immortal soul spilling out, too. What would it look like? Would the soul be as pop-eyed as the man himself?

She did not like her father's friend. And he did not like her.

"She is disfigured," he told her father the next day as they lay in a grass house with room only for the three of them, like sticks of wood in a row. Beyond the open door, this tribe celebrated around a fire, dancing and drinking yellow tea, shouting in a language Teresa did not understand. Half their faces were painted blue, the other half white.

"The tattoos are bad enough," Alonso del Castillo went on. "But you let them put a board under her head when she was a baby. The back of her head is flat."

"It is their custom," Teresa's father said. "Her mother insisted."

"But how can she be a Christian now? How can she meet the Redeemer?"

"Because of a flat head?" Her father sighed with exasperation. In the darkness, he stroked Teresa's hair. "Go to sleep," he told her.

"No, I have thought about these things," Alonso del Castillo continued. "Heaven will not admit men or women or children who are no longer in the image of our Maker. Heaven will not admit a man, for example, who has tattooed himself about the face and chest, or who has altered himself in other ways."

"Alonso," her father said. "We are tired."

But Teresa noticed that he touched his own chest, where her uncle had once inserted a reed two palms long and one finger thick. She realized now that the reed was gone. Teresa couldn't think back to when this had happened, when her father had removed the reed. So much was happening now, a blur of movement, cures, prayer, and dance.

This time, when they left the large and prosperous village, most of the men and half the women traveled with them, all the way to the next village, where they were given deer meat to eat. When this village came forward to be cured, the people first put on the ground their bows and arrows, sandals and beads, red ochre and seashell jewelry, and the men and women who had come with the Christians took these things for themselves—even before a single person could be healed or blessed.

From then on, it was a constant exchange. The people from one tribe accompanied the healers to the next and from that tribe took all their goods. The people who were newly rich stayed behind or returned home, while those who had lost their belongings accompanied the Christians and the Moor to the next village and had their turn.

Her father called it robbery. Dorantes worried that some villagers would become angry and enslave them. But no one did. Each time, the four healers were welcomed with smiles and celebrations. "It is a drama," the Moor finally decided, "like the processions you have in Spain. Each village plays its part. Each man gets what he has lost. It is a form of trade as well as religion. They call us the Children of the Sun since we only walk in that direction. They call us shamans or medicine men."

Alonso del Castillo moaned. "The Inquisition has burned people for less."

The three other men ignored him, as usual.

"But they treat us more like prisoners," Andrés Dorantes complained.

Teresa's father agreed that they had become valuable. No one could speak to the healers without permission from their guides. No one could eat food until the healers had blessed it. Sometimes this meant the four men had to spend a long time making the sign of the Cross over each piece of dried fruit and meat, and even Alonso del Castillo had to help with this job although he worried endlessly that it was another sacrilege. Teresa's father only grinned and winked at her. The important thing was that they were walking west, toward New Spain. The important thing was to avoid another winter in the desert.

Sometimes Teresa thought about her foster mother, whom she could no longer remember very well. More rarely, she thought about her mother, whom she could not remember at all, only a smell of fish and salt and blackberries. She thought about how far they had walked, past mesquite and scrub brush and cactus. They had crossed tumbling streams and one wide river—the Moor had carried Teresa on his shoulders—and she had seen mountains for the first time and had loved them instantly, the way they made so many different shapes, the way they changed and shifted with the light. She could feel their eyes following her as she trotted beside her father, holding his hand. She knew they wondered what she would do next.

Each day, her father waited for signs of what he called civilization. After one feast at yet another village, a hugely fat woman showed the Moor two painted gourds decorated with feathers. When the woman shook these gourds, the pebbles inside rattled like rain, the sound of water and power, the sound of water returning to the sea. The Moor translated what the woman said. "These gourds have a special magic. They come floating down the river."

Teresa no longer understood any language but Spanish, for she spoke only to her father and occasionally to his three friends. But the Moor was good at using sign and at understanding the different dialects of the tribes. He shook the gourds again.

"They are too big to be wild," Dorantes declared. "Someone grew these. Do you remember the fields we saw in *La Florida*?"

Her father also shook the gourds, and Teresa heard the magic as loud as a clap of thunder. The pebbles rattled. The water rushed to sea. Teresa reached for a gourd, for she wanted to hold that sound. She needed to hold it, and her body lifted, light with desire. She floated up, just a bit, into the air. But her father said no, and the hugely fat woman laughed.

Only a few days later, in a place where the people dressed in long leather skirts and leather aprons, the leader gave Dorantes a bell of copper decorated with a cat's face. This bell was brighter than the little copper bells her father had once given Teresa's grandparents. In fact, her father told Teresa, this copper was of superior quality, surprisingly pure. He and his friends began to whisper about gold, a yellow metal even better than copper.

Now when they moved on, they were followed by more people than ever before, so many they stretched out in a long line. Her father exclaimed that he saw over two thousand men, women, and children. With his hands and fingers, he tried to show Teresa how big that number was. She nodded. She could see for herself.

To help feed this crowd, the men who had arrows and bows went up into the mountains nearby and brought back deer, five or six at a time. If they found a herd of peccary, they slaughtered all of them. Hunters also traveled ahead of the group, carrying curved throwing sticks that they used to kill hares. Sometimes they made a sport in which they drove the animal from bush to bush, hunter to hunter, until the frightened creature ran straight into a human hand.

As darkness sifted through the tall yucca plants, Teresa and her father would climb a rise and watch the campfires below. The lights flickered on the ground like fallen stars. The nights were cold, and the people used the fires for warmth and comfort, sitting idly around the dying coals, nibbling on prickly pear, juniper berries, and piñon nuts. Sometimes they roasted a small animal they had caught during the day. Usually they simply sat doing nothing, eating nothing, saying nothing. They sat amazed, just like Teresa, just like her father, wondering what miracle the next day would bring.

3

Teresa wasn't often afraid. She had her father. She had the Moor. But that day, her father was so angry, shouting at Andrés Dorantes and Alonso del Castillo. The guides also looked angry, their bodies tense. They had just refused to take the Children of the Sun farther west. They said the land was too desolate, without food or water. Also, the villages west of here were the homes of their enemies, bad people who did not deserve to be blessed or healed. Instead they would guide the healers north to friendly villages.

"Then we will go alone, without you," her father said in Spanish and in sign, motioning to himself and then to the set-ting sun. Spittle glistened in his gray and brown beard.

"Wait," Alonso del Castillo murmured. "How can we find our way alone?'

"This is not the time to lose faith, Alonso," her father scolded.

"Let us stay calm," the Moor suggested.

But her father's face was growing red. "We will go forward! We will not stop! We are being led by Christ Himself!"

Dorantes looked at the Indians, who each carried a bow and a quiver of arrows. "Remember where we are," Dorantes warned.

That night, Teresa woke to a desert silvered by the moon. Cries came from the people sitting around the campfires, for three men had died of a sudden illness, three hunters esteemed by their tribe. In the morning, the people from this group stood before the ramada of grass mats where Teresa and her father and the other Children of the Sun slept. The women had already cut their faces, mixing blood with ash and dirt. No one looked directly at Cabeza de Vaca but spoke to the side of his body, as though addressing an invisible presence there. Now they would take the healers wherever they wanted to go.

"What have you done?" Alonso del Castillo whispered, his liquid-brown eyes bulging even more than usual.

Her father waited for the Indians to move away. "I haven't done anything," he whispered back, hugging Teresa closer to him. "There has always been sickness in this camp. These men died because they were sick. Do you think I wanted that? Do you think I have the power to harm men?"

Alonso del Castillo moaned and turned away, and from that point on, the people who traveled with them believed the Christians could cause death by willing it. Also, the guides were walking into the land of their enemies, and when they reached a village, they said goodbye to the healers and left quickly the same day. Now the men and women and children of that village did not run out smiling but stayed inside their mud houses, seated on the ground, faces to the wall. All their property was placed on the floor, ready to be taken. But these farmers did not have much to give. Little rain had fallen in the last two years, and even wild plants like mesquite and prickly pear had no fruit. The people signed to the Spaniards: nothing in the sky loves us anymore.

Teresa trailed behind her father, west through the desert, accompanied by only a few followers. Each morning, Cabeza de Vaca gave everyone a handful of grass seeds and roots and ate a handful himself. By late afternoon, when Teresa became too weak to walk, the Moor would carry her. "More water," she begged, but the Moor only shrugged.

One day, they stumbled down a hill to see a line of deep blue gleaming at the horizon. They all began to run. As if she were dreaming, Teresa heard the sound of waves lapping against sand. She felt the stir of memory. She saw an upturned mouth and gold flecks around each iris. Her father grabbed her, shouting in a hoarse voice, "Look, Teresa! We did it! We have walked all the way to the South Sea!" He knelt and began to pray, "Thank you, Our Lord, for your guidance. Thank you for your magnificence and glory! We ask fervently, with tears of joy and sorrow, that you show us the way back to the arms of the church and our most compassionate King."

Looking up, he motioned at Teresa to kneel, too, and she did, happy to be beside him again on a wind-swept beach.

They turned south and east because the people by the sea were very poor, with hardly anything to eat. Every day, Teresa watched a range of mountains watching her. At the end of the range, a fang-toothed mountain stood apart like a man or woman standing apart from a crowd, looking straight at Teresa. By the time they were at the foot of this fang-toothed mountain, they had entered the country of the Opatas, an impossibly wealthy tribe who grew fields of yellow maize and green-leafed beans, with shirts made of soft dyed cotton cloth and villages of grand houses built of stone and adobe. As before, fabulous stories ran ahead of the healers, and large groups followed them to the next village, where they were given food and supplies. Most of these villagers chose to return home, but others stayed to join the Children of the Sun, their numbers once again increasing.

At each place, her father asked if the people had seen other men like himself, with long noses and hairy faces. Finally one leader said that a wise woman just outside his village had something that may have come from such men.

"What is this something?" Dorantes asked.

The man shrugged and spoke to the Moor, who translated. "We do not see this woman often. She is a healer like you, but she lives alone on a hill we do not like to climb. She is strange and makes us nervous."

"Show me the way," Teresa's father commanded.

Dorantes, the Moor, and her father strode ahead, following their guides up the slope of the hill and talking all the while. Teresa lagged behind. Deliberately, she lingered, wanting to be alone.

She couldn't understand why the people here did not like to climb this hill. For it delighted her! The plants were nothing out of the ordinary: thorny mesquite and catclaw, the prickly pear she had eaten all her life, the humped cactus and long-limbed cactus, tall yellow grass, and summer flowers—white daisies, purple asters, orange poppies. The plants were common, nothing out of the ordinary, but on this hill they were much louder than Teresa had ever heard before. She listened to their musical rings, a sharp ding-a-ling for the sunflower, a milder note for the blue phlox. Behind the flowers, trees hummed and bushes murmured, songs of growing and leafing and rooting. The hill was a celebration of sound.

Teresa tried to concentrate on the animals, the chatter of mice and packrats, hares and rabbits. Though she had heard their voices before, the images they sent were stronger here and much clearer. If she focused on one particular animal, she could enter its very thoughts.

A young coyote whimpered alone in his den, his mother gone hunting. Awake and restless, the pup snarled: come back, come back. Come back and I'll bite you. I'll grab your muzzle. I'll hold on! The pup twisted and chewed his tail. I'll come find you, he decided. I'll surprise you!

Teresa shushed the animal. Wait there, she said sternly. Don't go outside without your mother.

The coyote startled and put his paws over his face.

By now, her father was far ahead, and Teresa stopped. The earth whispered through the soles of her sandals made of yucca rope. Listen, the earth said. We have a song for you. Teresa listened. Yes, she could hear them, veins of silver singing through rock. Limestone hissing with the sound of waves. Boulders of lava remembering fire. They were all talking. Most stones said the same thing again and again and again, finding that one thing of great interest, repeating themselves and content with that.

"Teresa!" her father called from above. Teresa held up her hand, wanting him to be quiet. "Teresa!" her father called and laughed at how pensively she stood. "Hurry now. We are waiting for you." He was in a good mood, on the trail of this something left behind by men like himself, Spanish *hidalgos* who had passed this way perhaps recently. "Come on, precious girl. Stay in my sight."

The house where the wise woman lived was large, a rambling adobe built on top of the hill. Teresa saw that the walls were crumbling and the roof sagged. Nearby, a weedy garden looked half-dead, the odor of rotting fruit in the air. Just outside the house, the leader of the village stopped and shouted to let the old woman know she had visitors. When there was no reply, he shrugged and told the Children of the Sun to sit and wait. Dorantes grumbled that he did not want to wait, that he was thirsty, that he was hungry. Her father only nodded, willing to show another healer his respect.

The time passed quickly for Teresa as she lay on the earth and listened to what the hill had to say—the questions of a darkling beetle, the complicated story of an owl watching them from a mesquite. This place was so loud, so rich with voices. Teresa felt she could lie here forever.

As was his custom, the Moor took the opportunity to nap, shading his forehead with one black hand. The leader of the village also closed his eyes. Only her father and Dorantes sat and did nothing and grew bored. By the time the wise woman emerged from the doorway, both men were impatient.

The woman looked older than anyone Teresa had ever seen. Her face creased into a web of wrinkles. Her braided hair was bone-white, her eyes black, her skin and teeth a light brown. Slightly stooped, she had dressed in a cotton loincloth and nothing more. Over her shrunken breasts, around her neck, she wore a seashell necklace, white like her hair, with gleams of coral pink.

In the language of his tribe, the leader introduced them. The Moor whispered in her father's ear and then spoke to the woman. She nodded without warmth and motioned for them to enter her home.

The world was cooler inside, dim and musty. The smell of something rotting lingered here, too, and Teresa wrinkled her nose. The old woman seemed indifferent to the matter of where her visitors would sit, and so they stood while she lowered herself onto a mat of woven yucca rope.

"What is this thing?" Dorantes asked in Spanish. "What does this witch have that we want?"

The leader looked sharply at him, and her father pulled his friend's arm. "Quiet," Cabeza de Vaca said. "Can't you feel it? She is . . . she has . . . something important."

Her father sounded eager, and the wise woman peered at him more closely than before. Grunting, she shifted her thighs as if to struggle again to her feet. Then she sighed, sank bank, and instead spoke to the leader, who nodded and suddenly left the house. The Moor went with him, while Teresa's father and Dorantes stood awkwardly as the woman seemed to doze.

Teresa tried to see into the shadows of the room, where a cooking pot stood against the outline of a hearth. Clay pots lined up against the wall, and bundles of plants hung from the ceiling. A spotted animal skin lay crumpled on the floor.

Teresa craned her neck to see what it was. A blocky head with yellow eyes glared at her.

But now the leader returned, the Moor behind him, carrying a pole. "She was using it as a scarecrow." The Moor grinned. "Out in her corn field."

On top of the pole perched a gleaming object, its silver showing through the dirt and leaves. To her surprise, Teresa recognized the magic hat almost immediately. This was exactly what her father had described to her, what the conquistadors wore when they fought against their enemies. Spears and knives could not pierce this hat, which was meant to shine in the sun and frighten the wicked. From the helmet, four horseshoe nails and the buckle from a sword belt also dangled, tied on with yucca thread.

Dorantes grabbed the magic hat and wrestled it off the pole. "Where did you get this?" he demanded, as if this were his house and he the master.

The wise woman just looked at him. The leader spoke to the Moor, who said, "It came from the south. A man brought it to her before he died."

"What did the man say?" Teresa's father knelt before the woman, radiating charm, all his good will and peaceful intentions. "How far south?" he coaxed. "Don't be afraid. Tell us what the man said."

The wise woman smiled for the first time. Again she spoke to the leader, who spoke to the Moor, who said, "He was dying of a wound in his leg that had turned black. The man who had killed him sat on a giant deer and had hair on his face like you, like the Children of the Sun. There were other men, on giant deer, who carried long knives that they used to murder two boys. They tried to capture this man but he escaped."

At this news, Dorantes gave a glad shout, "They are close by!"

Her father rose and nodded. Teresa knew he was also glad, with just a bit of sorrow for the man and two boys who had died.

The wise woman glanced at Teresa and closed her eyes, as if tired of so many people crowded into her dark and cluttered adobe house. She lifted her hand and turned it palm out. Teresa stared. Then the wise woman whispered to the leader of the village. When he shrugged, she whispered again, and the leader spoke to the Moor, who translated, "What you have lost will be restored to you."

The wise woman looked straight at Cabeza de Vaca, and Teresa felt a shiver of energy up her spine. She felt suddenly lonely and went to lean against her father's leg. Once he, too, had ridden a horse and carried a long knife. He, too, had worn a magic hat. The future and past were racing toward each other, and the wind they made prickled the hairs on the back of her neck.

4

Teresa could feel the weight on her shoulders, the sorrow on the land, as soon it became clear that the Spanish traveling this southern country were slave hunters, capturing people to work in the King's silver mines. Her father no longer looked so happy. In most villages, the slavers took half the men and all the women and children, burning the grass houses or dragging them apart with their horses. Those who escaped wandered the hills, afraid to return home. Everywhere now, people crept about frightened and depressed, hiding in the woods and canyons. Over and over, her father promised the refugees that he would find the Spanish conquistadors and tell them to stop. When they heard these promises, many of the people looked hopeful. They signed back to the Moor: ask about my sister. Ask about my mother.

Dorantes worried their new followers would blame the Children of the Sun for what the slavers were doing. "Eventually these people will turn on us," he said.

"They think of us as healers, men from Heaven," her father argued. "They treat us with kindness, giving us whatever they have. We must go forward."

"If we can," Dorantes worried. "There are no crops. No one has planted food."

"We are so close," Teresa's father said. "Can't you feel it?"

The very next day, their group came across four wooden stakes left in the ground. Flies buzzed in the afternoon air. "They tied their horses here," her father said to Dorantes. "We have to hurry!"

But most of the people who traveled with them could not hurry but only walk slowly out of grief and hunger. Andrés Dorantes and Alonso del Castillo also sat down and declared they were too weak to move another league—or even half a league. Her father decided that he and the Moor would go ahead, with just a few guides. "Of course," he said to Teresa. "You will come with me."

They walked quickly, almost running, through the scrubby oak, twisted juniper trees, and prickly pear. A black raven followed them, its gurgly *kro-ak, kro-ak* insistent from the stunted pines. Now the bird flew ahead and croaked from another thin-leafed bush. Teresa tried to listen, to understand. The raven cawed and flapped its black wings. *Kro-ak! Kro-ak!*

First, the Moor saw hoof prints in the sand. Then at the top of a gravel rise, four men on horseback stood outlined against the blue sky. The Spaniards saw Cabeza de Vaca and his guides, too, and the horses stopped walking. With the sun in her eyes, Teresa tried to count the shadowed shapes. She stepped forward, ready to run toward the animals her father had talked about so lovingly. But a pressure held her back. It was the Moor's heavy hand.

Her father was the one to move and speak. His voice shrilled, "I am Álvar Núñez Cabeza de Vaca. I am Álvar Núñez Cabeza de Vaca! I am Álvar Núñez Cabeza de Vaca, grandson of Pedro de Vera, treasurer of the Pánfilo de Narváez expedition, a loyal subject of King Charles the Fifth!"

The long knives swung and pointed down the hill. The horses shifted. The Spanish men on horseback were silent. They looked huge, dressed in bulky clothes of leather, metal, and thick padded cloth. Teresa recognized what her father called armor, the layers of a hammered gleaming material. Her father had explained to her all the parts of this costume, and she knew the words in Spanish—for helmet, for lance, for breastplate. Still, she had never imagined that her father's friends would be quite this monstrous, their hats burning silver in the white sun, high on their horses on the gravel slope.

Her father faced them dressed in a cloth around his waist. His gray hair and beard flew about his naked chest as he climbed up toward the men. One of them bent his arm as though to throw his long knife. Her father laughed like a woman, his voice oddly pitched. "Are you going to kill a miracle? Are you going to kill a man who has spent so many years trying to find you?"

Teresa's father kept laughing as he moved with his arms stretched out, and the man lowered his lance and spoke in Spanish, as did the other men, whispers at first and then exclamations. Her father laughed as though he couldn't stop while the sweat-blotched horses lifted their feet, stepping back and stepping forward, unable to run with their heads pulled up so tightly by the reins.

Now one horse lifted its tail and ejected plops of wet, grassy-smelling feces. Caught in the Moor's grip, Teresa waited impatiently. With their long bony faces and big yellow teeth, these animals were amazingly unattractive. Yet her father had always described them as beautiful. He had described them with such tenderness. The Moor held her shoulder, not letting her go. The Opata guides behind the Moor murmured to each other, alarmed to be so close to the Spanish slavers.

"Eight years!" Her father yelled at the Moor. "It is 1536, Esteban. Eight years!" He spoke again to the men on horses. "We must go to the captain now!" Then he turned back, still yelling, as though she and the Moor had gone deaf. "Come on! Keep everyone together! Follow us!"

Teresa understood that this was one of the most important moments of her father's life. This was comparable to meeting

Charles the Fifth, the King of Spain. This would equal the day he had stood beside Pánfilo de Narváez and sailed toward the New World. Everything about this moment—the grassy smell of the horses, the glint of sun on the silver helmets, the sound of Spanish spoken by a stranger—all this was something her father would remember and keep, a form of treasure.

The captain was only a short distance away, surrounded by more men on horseback. Also dressed in armor, he dismounted heavily and took her father and the Moor to speak under the shade of a pine tree. The Moor still kept his hand on Teresa's shoulder. "Be quiet now," the black man whispered in her ear. "Be careful, darling. Do what I do."

"Are these your Indians?" the captain spoke eagerly, staring at the guides. On the ground, he stood much shorter than her father. His Spanish was different, too, and hard for Teresa to understand. "Where did you get them? Are there more?"

Her father explained that the people with him were friends and companions, not slaves. He had other friends, too . . .

The captain interrupted, "We have had terrible luck." His dark nervous eyes swept across Teresa and the Moor and noted them with interest. "This country is empty. Everyone is gone. My men are getting hungry."

After a confusing time, with more interruptions, Teresa's father managed to say that two other Spanish gentlemen from the Pánfilo de Narváez expedition were waiting a few leagues east, with a large group of natives who carried baskets of dried fruit and maize. These villagers were also friends and companions. They would be happy to share what food they had.

At this good news, the captain opened his mouth wide to show stumps of rotting teeth. He grabbed Teresa's father and hugged him hard against the shiny metal on his chest, truly welcoming him for the first time. With a cry, her father slumped into the other man's embrace. The Moor grinned.

Now the captain sent his men to fetch Andrés Dorantes and Alonso del Castillo, and in the afternoon of the next day, the two Children of the Sun came with all the people who had been gathered around them. These were the families, widows and orphans, brothers and sisters, daughters and sons who had been hiding from the Spanish slave hunters these last few months. "You will not be harmed," her father told them as he helped the slavers take the baskets of dried fruit and maize. "You will be allowed to return to your homes. You will be allowed to grow crops again." Patiently he went among the fearful men and women, touching this person and that one as he was used to doing, blessing the few children. The Moor and Teresa stayed close to his side.

Suddenly, and as if by plan, the Spanish sitting high on their horses spread out in a circle around the villagers. Outside the circle, Andrés Dorantes and Alonso del Castillo lay sprawled exhausted on the ground. For the moment, the captain seemed to have disappeared. Her father whispered to the Moor the same thing, again and again, urging him to repeat it. "Tell them they can return home. Tell them they will not be harmed. When they go back to their villages, they must give thanks to God and Christ, our Redeemer. They must give thanks and plant their fields."

The Moor signed this to the waiting crowd, silent and surrounded. The baskets of food were already fastened to the Christians' saddlebags.

"Captain!" Her father spoke with obvious relief when he saw the man arrive. "I must speak with you."

This time, the captain did not dismount. Nodding in a stern way and sitting very straight in his saddle, he towered over her father and the Moor. Teresa watched his horse breathe, strands of slobber moving in and out of the black nostrils. The long brown flank was wet with sweat. As Teresa stared into the gold-flecked eyes of the captain's horse, she suddenly knew what her father meant when he had described his mare as beautiful. This horse looked at Teresa with such intelligence, as if he already knew and trusted her. Teresa longed to reach out and stroke his furred neck.

May I touch you? she asked the horse.

The animal moved back in surprise. Irritated, the captain jerked the rope at the horse's mouth. Who are you? the horse questioned.

"I am sending you to the Governor of this province," the captain was saying to her father. "You will be treated well. You will be safe! Good-bye! Godspeed!"

Smiling, the captain yanked even harder at the reins, so that the horse was forced to turn quickly. "But what about these people?" her father shouted as he grabbed at the same leather rope. The eyes of the horse rolled in white half-moons. The captain pulled the rope back viciously and shrieked, "I'm letting you keep the girl, remember! And the Moor!"

The horse twirled. Dust flew up in Teresa's face. Out of the dust, other men came to herd her and her father and the Moor toward Alonso del Castillo and Andrés Dorantes. By now, the villagers were packed together ever more closely, guarded by the slave hunters on horses and their long knives. This had happened very fast, all in a moment. The crowd began to moan as the healers and Teresa were led away.

Her father was trying to weep. His face contorted, but his eyes were dry and he held Teresa's hand, hurting her fingers. A black raven cawed behind them. Teresa tried to listen. The earth watched the scene with great interest. I will still love you, the earth whispered. I will still be with you.

They traveled for two weeks to the Governor's house. The Spanish slavers would not carry them on their horses, and so they had to walk the entire way. Her father and the Moor were unusually quiet, and Dorantes and Castillo also spoke little, except to complain about the lack of food.

Everything changed when they passed through the large wooden gates into a courtyard of cobbled stone and trees full of hanging fruit. Sprays of red flowers covered the whitewashed adobe walls that seemed to go on for leagues in every direction. Two slave hunters escorted them up marble steps to a carved door that led into a huge room with enormous pieces of furniture. Teresa remembered the stories her father had told her about his home in Seville.

The Governor himself came to greet them. Teresa's father still held her hand.

"Pánfilo de Narváez!" The Governor was round and smiling.

"The treasurer of that expedition," her father corrected and bowed. "I am Álvar Núñez Cabeza de Vaca."

"We welcome you and your companions! It is a miracle! After so many years! And I believe you have much to tell us."

The Governor and her father spoke there in the room of enormous furniture, and the Governor hugged each of the men, except the Moor. Finally they were all taken through the main hall with its high ceiling and colored pictures. Teresa wanted to stop, for these paintings of men and women, plants and animals, were so lifelike, so wonderful. She could have stared at them for hours. They went past another room, also bigger than a grass house, with a long piece of raised wood—a table, Teresa thought—covered by white cloth and metal tools. They passed one extraordinary object after another. Then the Governor left, and an Opata woman took them up a steep staircase. She led Teresa and her father to another wooden door.

Teresa's father pushed her gently inside the small room. "Someone will bring you food," he said and pushed her back again. "No, you have to stay here. I will come to you later."

Teresa stared about the windowless square with a pallet on the floor. "What do you mean?" she asked. "Why can't I go with you?"

38

Many hours later, the Moor brought her a plate of beans and meat and slices of orange fruit. "They are having a feast at the Governor's table," the Moor told her, sitting cross-legged on the floor. "All the important people are eating with your father tonight. Everyone wants to hear about the places we traveled and whether or not there was gold in the villages."

"What is this?" Teresa pointed angrily at the orange fruit.

The Moor praised the sweetness of cantaloupe and explained that she was to wait in this little room always until someone came for her. She should never wander about the Governor's house alone. She should never disturb the peace of the Governor's house. Her father and Alonso del Castillo and Andrés Dorantes were nearby, each in his private bedroom. Of course, their bedrooms were elegantly furnished with two carved chairs, a wardrobe, and a mirror from Spain. Each *hidalgo* had a servant to help him dress and prepare for the day.

No, the Moor said, she could not stay with her father. The Governor would think it very wrong for her father, Cabeza de Vaca, to have an Indian child next to him in his bed. The priest would certainly not allow it. Yes, the Moor said, they had already seen a priest named Fray Tomás. This had been the cause of much simpering and sighing, especially from Alonso del Castillo.

Now Teresa was surprised to learn that the Moor himself was a slave again. He had been brought on the ships from Spain to serve his master Andrés Dorantes, and for this reason, he would be staying in the stables outside and not in the house.

"Most of the people you see here are servants," the Moor explained, "who are like slaves but who must be treated more kindly. The slaves work in the silver mines where they are very much needed, for this is where the Spanish get their wealth. But I will not be sent to the mines. I am too valuable now. I know too many things about what lies to the north."

The black man gave her a little pot for her urine, and then he left. Teresa didn't know what to do. She had never slept alone in her life.

Her father pointed. "*Un escritorio*," he spoke reverently, as though talking about a sacred object. The writing desk was a high box of wood carved with the faces of Spanish men, their helmets framed by flowers and leaves. A metal key dangled from a string attached to the top of the desk. When her father inserted the key into a hole, the front of the *escritorio* fell open like a mouth, which made Teresa exclaim and step back. Inside, more boxes could be pulled out. They were inlaid, her father said, in the Moorish style with ivory and tortoiseshell. Most importantly, the wooden lid came down, and on this a man could put his parchment paper, pot of ink, and feather pen. He could write here, and he could read.

As he took Teresa on a tour of his bedroom, her father also made her pause before the carved wooden chairs with vines crawling up their legs. He tried to show her how a lady would sit in such a chair. At this point, however, he hesitated, confessing some ignorance about the matter.

Lying on the bed, dressed in new embroidered pants and a cotton shirt, Andrés Dorantes laughed in a nasty way.

"Shut up," her father said. With another metal key, he opened the lock to the wardrobe, where his clothes were folded and stored. Teresa put her head into the closet and breathed in the smell of sweet wood. Then her father locked the wardrobe and made her open it. Her fingers fumbled. But her father waited as though he trusted her completely to accomplish this very necessary task. Finally, the tall thin doors swung apart. "Bravo!" her father said. "Excellent!"

"Bravo!" Dorantes echoed. "You are teaching her well to become a housekeeper in your mansion in Seville."

"Shut up," her father said again as he watched Teresa examine herself in the tall heavy mirror. Teresa could see him watching, standing behind her, yet also in front of her in the glass. This was amusing, and she smiled. Smiling, she opened her mouth, leaning close to the mirror and trying to look down into her throat. Like the ripples of a pond, this mirror had distortions, although the shiny surface was clearer and brighter than any pond she had ever seen. Teresa touched the blue lines tattooed on each cheek. She clapped her hands against her thighs, as did the girl across from her.

"Yes, your wife will be pleased with this little one," Dorantes continued. "No doubt it will spark her imagination. She will wonder about all your adventures in the New World."

"Shut up," Teresa's father said for the third time.

But Dorantes only sat up and spoke more urgently, "A woman expects to wait for her husband, Álvar, especially when he uses her family's wealth to go to the Indies. But she does not expect him to bring home a bastard as her reward."

"Listen to me," her father used his most formal tone. "From this point on, consider yourself barred from talking about my wife. The topic is closed to you."

"She will have enemies," Dorantes continued with hardly a pause, and Teresa knew that the "she" he spoke of was not her father's wife in Spain. "There are people waiting to discredit our journey and everything we say. There are priests who will wonder about the healings we performed. There is the Inquisition still! Alonso is right about that. Heretics are still being burned! We have no gold or silver to pacify these men. You will have enemies, and they will be her enemies, and they will use her easily for their purposes."

"My father can protect me," Teresa interrupted. She hated Dorantes. She wished she knew a good curse.

"Of course, I can." Her father nodded. He put his hand on the top of her head and moved it down against the flatness at

41

the back. "Although Andrés is also right," he said softly. "You have to learn, as you have already learned, to be clever and quiet and to suffer all indignities in silence. I will not always be there to help."

Now Alonso del Castillo appeared in the doorway. He also was dressed in new clothes that covered his scabby splotched skin. His beard had been trimmed, and a pearl dangled from one ear. "What is she doing here?" he asked with distaste. "We have to talk."

"There is no harm in her staying," Teresa's father soothed.

"She hears too much. She remembers too much."

"You worry about everything," her father said.

"But I agree with Alonso." Dorantes stood and crossed to the hallway. "Hey," he yelled to a servant woman passing by. "Take this girl with you, back to her room."

Later it would seem that everything happened at that moment. The rest of Teresa's life was planned and revealed at that moment when her father hung his head and let the servant woman take her away.

In truth, of course, many more weeks passed. One morning, the Moor left with a group of men. Dorantes had sold him to the Governor to lead an expedition north in search of villages where the streets were paved with gold. Her father had been shocked, but the Moor didn't seem to mind. He had grown to enjoy traveling with his magical painted gourds, astounding the villagers who crowded around him, especially the women. Teresa watched him leave, standing with her father by an open window. Grinning, the black man waved at her.

Later she tried to think what she could have said or done during this time. How could it have happened differently? She knew it had something to do with this house, with the carved chairs and wardrobe, with the *escritorio* and its inlaid drawers of tortoiseshell and ivory. She knew it had something to do with Andrés Dorantes and Alonso del Castillo and the Governor.

She knew what her father meant to do, knew in the center of her body, that spot between the rib cage and stomach, which is why she was awake one early morning when the pink light slanted east through the fruit trees in the courtyard.

This time he did not come to take her away. He did not pause at the small dark room and whisper, "Hush, put your legs around me. We have to go."

Naked, without her new cotton dress, Teresa ran down the stairway, through the large terrifying hall, onto the front steps where she was never allowed to walk without permission. She stopped naked on the cold flagstone of the courtyard. Guards shouted to each other as they opened the wooden gate to let the group of riders pass through.

Teresa saw her father on a bay mare. All his gifts from the Governor had been loaded on the horse behind him. She saw Andrés Dorantes on another horse, gesturing with his hand to a rider at his side. Alonso del Castillo gestured back. The guards shouted to each other. The horses made their own noises, striking hooves on the cobblestones, wheezing and whistling.

Teresa knew where they were going. To Mexico City and the sailing port of Vera Cruz. "Papá!" she screamed.

Her father turned his head.

"Papá!" Teresa flew, then stumbled on a step in the flagstone.

A hand caught and held her back. A gardener picking fruit from the trees held her with one arm. No, he said in horror. She should not run after the gentlemen leaving for their ship. He scolded her in the language of the Indians here.

Her father turned his head.

Teresa screamed, "Papá!"

Her father said something. He rose in his saddle, saying something sad and regretful. She could read his intent as always. His love for her flowed from his hand into the air, straight to her, touching her cheek. She would be fine. They would take care of her. This was better for her and for him. She would always be unwelcome in Spain. She would always be a danger in Spain. She belonged here. He had made arrangements. Someday he would come back for her.

"Papá!" Teresa cried.

The riders kicked the horses, who pushed past the guards. The guards, with their helmets, armor, and lances, closed the gate. The courtyard was silent except for the gardener, still scolding.

The pulse of Teresa's heart beat strongly in her neck. The ground under her feet softened and shuddered, and she remembered the story she had once been told: the earth was a giant turtle walking slowly through an empty sky. The earth was a giant turtle walking so slowly and so carefully that the people on its back did not fall off.

Teresa saw the turtle pause. She saw the turtle move its long neck, looking back and lifting up awkwardly. If the turtle lifted high enough, if the turtle shook its back hard enough, the land would tilt until everyone tumbled into nothingness, until all the people, all the villages, all the men and women and children, Spanish and Indian, Christian and Moor, tumbled into that empty sky.

Teresa stood in the silence of the Governor's courtyard. She saw the turtle lift and shake its heavy back. She waited for the world to end.

5

Her father left, the world did not end, and Teresa stopped speaking. Her tongue fell back in her throat and held itself apart. For a few days, she cried all the time. Her eyelids swelled, and her face felt bruised. When she wasn't crying, she was listening. She listened for the hooves of her father's horse to return on the cobbled courtyard. When nothing happened, when her father didn't return, she stopped listening, too.

Her father had made arrangements. He had gone to Fray Tomás at the last possible moment, explaining how he had to leave his young servant behind. Her father had stressed that last word, his beloved *servant*, this poor, deformed, tattooed child from the north. The friar had promised to take charge of Teresa. He would teach her Spanish history and culture. He would prepare her for marriage.

Now the Franciscan monk wanted Teresa to go to school. The Governor's house stood on the edge of a large village with houses for the Spanish slave hunters and their families, the servants and slaves, the shopkeepers and blacksmiths and artisans. The village also had a church with a separate building for Fray Tomás and a classroom for a dozen Indian boys and girls. Although the girls worked mainly at their embroidery, they could also spend an hour each morning learning to read.

"Unfortunately," the monk said to the Governor's house-keeper, his long white hands resting on Teresa's shoulders, "the girl is mute. She cannot speak."

"But, no," the housekeeper studied Teresa. "I heard her chattering myself when she first came with the gentlemen."

The housekeeper was stocky, with muscular arms and thick legs, an Indian whose family had worked generations for the Aztecs, the former rulers of Mexico. She worked now just the same for the Spanish. Teresa stared up at the woman's face. The broad brown cheeks, flat nose, and wide forehead were scarred with the craters of smallpox, as though the housekeeper had been attacked by a man flicking a knife, cutting here and there bits of flesh from her skin.

"Then is she unwilling? Teresa, are you unwilling?" Fray Tomás knelt and turned Teresa around so he could look at her directly. His pale cheeks and thin nose were oily and pimpled, his beard a wisp of blond-brown hair. "Teresa," he said with some distress, "you must speak if you want me to help you. Do you want to learn to embroider and read like the girls in my school? Do you want to learn your catechism and the ways of Christ, Our Lord? Do you want to serve Our Lord?"

She could not hear him.

"I think she is also deaf." The friar looked up at the house-keeper. "What can I do? I promised the Governor's guest that I would watch over this child, his beloved servant. He made me swear to him the most holy of oaths. But what can I do?"

"Leave the girl with me," the housekeeper replied, shrug-ging her big shoulders. "She is how old? Seven or eight? A good age. I'll take care of her."

That morning, Teresa began her work under the eye of an assistant cook under the eye of the cook under the eye of the housekeeper. Obediently, her feet carried her to a pile of recently plucked wild duck, ready to be cut up for soup. Her fingers learned to hold a knife and chop between the gristle and bone. Duck fat and smoke coated her skin as she breathed in the brew of the low-ceilinged room filled with two stoves, two fireplaces, three tables for preparing food, and a half-dozen women moving about—a room filled with fire and meat, vegetables and talk, blood and knives. The assistant cooks were either kind or indifferent, giving her one chore after another, one long uneventful day of cutting up duck and turkey and cow and deer, chopping potatoes and onions, grinding maize, patting tortillas, tending fires, and sweeping floors. The work never ended but began again the next morning in a perfect circle. Teresa's hands did everything they were told to do. Her mouth did not speak or smile but only ate, for the food was plentiful. Teresa worked and ate and worked and ate. At night she slept with the other servants in an outside building near the horse stables.

Every week, Fray Tomás made sure she went to chapel. The pale young monk came for her personally and stood waiting at the kitchen door. All the kitchen servants had to go to Mass, but they could not go at the same time since the work was so constant and the chapel not large. Fray Tomás fetched Teresa for the earliest morning service, where she sat on a wooden bench with the other females, their black heads bent, their eyes sleepy. With a tender expression, the friar gave them the body of Christ to eat and His blood to drink. Long ago, Teresa had learned the prayers and responses from her father. But she couldn't hear them now, and she never said them out loud. She only stood and knelt as the others did, because Fray Tomás would be upset if she did not.

Almost always, the friar touched her hair and asked, "Are you happy, child? Are you well?" Almost always, Teresa nodded. She did not feel she was lying to him. She nodded because that is what he wanted her to do.

One morning, after three years of working in the kitchen, Teresa was told to follow the housekeeper up the wooden steps to the second floor. One of the girls who worked upstairs had died, and Teresa would now take her place. The housekeeper smiled as though conferring a great favor. They passed the door to Teresa's father's bedroom where he had opened the drawers inlaid in the Moorish style with ivory and tortoiseshell. They went into another room where the chairs also had vines crawling up their legs and an *escritorio* carved into the faces of Spanish *hidalgos*. Encouragingly, the housekeeper gave Teresa a dry cloth to wipe the chairs free of soot and dirt. When that was done to the housekeeper's satisfaction, she handed Teresa a second cloth dampened with oil. Now the housekeeper showed Teresa how to move her fingers in delicate circles, rubbing the curves of walnut until they darkened to black and the chair exuded a gleaming pleasure like an animal being stroked.

Under Teresa's touch, the carved vines seemed to extend their leaves and unfold with new growth. The vines seemed to flow out of the chair and wrap their tendrils around her hands. The vines seemed to hum and whisper, singing the green song of the earth. The song grew louder and louder, until Teresa fainted.

Surprised, the housekeeper had to carry the girl downstairs, put a wet rag on her face, and let her rest most of the day. Teresa was never asked to come upstairs again.

In all those years, of course, there was magic.

In the kitchen, they told the story of Juan Diego, an Aztec servant who had converted to Christianity after the conquest of Mexico City. One day on his way to Mass, Juan Diego heard music and saw a cloud of radiance from which the Mother Mary appeared in a mantle of blue-green, her skin as dark as his own skin. She spoke in the Aztec language, telling Juan to build a church honoring her. When the Bishop of Mexico City asked for a sign that this vision was true, Juan Diego left the Bishop's chamber and returned with his apron full of pink and white roses gathered impossibly in the middle of December.

The apron opened, the roses tumbled to the floor, and every-one could see that the cloth showed an image of The Blessed Lady, her feet resting on the moon of the old gods.

In the kitchen, they whispered of the dead child restored to life when his mother pressed a cross to his lips. They told how a medal of Saint Ignacio cured a woman of *viruela*, the smallpox. They knew of another poxed woman in labor for three days who gave birth to a healthy boy, without sores, after a priest had blessed her. They knew of a nun dressed in blue who could fly and a man who was saved from a bull by angels. They spoke of birds who talked and witches who would not drown.

Teresa was older now, taller than the housekeeper, her muscles strong and ropy. She bled every month, which meant she was a woman who could marry and bear children. She had spent more of her life in the Governor's kitchen, eight years chopping potatoes and wild duck, than she had traveling with her father and his friends. She still did not speak, and she often appeared not to listen. But in other ways she was obedient and—except for that time with the carved wooden chair—always completed her work.

One afternoon, she went to the herb garden to gather rosemary from the shrubs that grew into a low fragrant hedge. The housekeeper had noticed that Teresa was good with plants, bringing in the freshest leaves, cutting cleanly what the cook wanted, and not annoying the protective gardeners. Herbs were often needed in the kitchen and also to make sachets for the chests and wardrobes upstairs, some to keep away insects and mold, some to sweeten the air and bring back memories of Spain. The housekeeper only had to show Teresa once which plants to gather, at what time in the season, and which parts to use and why. After that, Teresa could be trusted to go to the garden alone.

The herb garden was large, broken into squares of yarrow and mint, sage and oregano, balm and lavender, their flowers buzzing in the spring and summer with a thousand bees, the air fluttering with a thousand butterflies.

"Teresa!" On the dirt path, Fray Tomás hurried toward her with his nervous gait, his bare feet seeming to run although he was not running. In the spring sunshine, he had pushed back his brown cowl, and moisture dampened his pale forehead and darkened the thin fringes of hair. The friar still looked young, but he was balding, which caused many jokes among the servants.

"I have something to show you," the monk said, stopping before Teresa and speaking loudly. His body odor threatened to overwhelm the rosemary. "In the Governor's library, we have the published journal of Cabeza de Vaca, his report to the King of Spain! Cabeza de Vaca, your former master. Do you remember him?"

The friar had decided that Teresa understood him best when he spoke with cheerful force and volume. He had also noticed that she heard those things that interested her. "It's a privilege," he shouted now. "The Governor has one of the most complete libraries in New Spain, although the Bishop may rival us in a few subjects. But we specialize in history and on matters that relate to the natives and to law. Your master's journal was published a few years ago. It took time for the ships to bring us a copy. You know what a book is, don't you, Teresa?"

She stared at him, holding the herbs close to her nose.

Fray Tomás squinted back guiltily, a guilt he kept alive for his own reasons. He had promised the Governor's guest, that kind and serious conquistador, to educate the girl and find her a husband. "But what can I do," he had told Teresa more than once, "when you will not speak and sometimes pretend not to hear? At least they no longer beat you for that. And you have become a good worker. The housekeeper says so! She is very fond of you."

Now the friar said, "I can show you this book if you want to see it. I can read you a few passages?"

Teresa stared, not able to move. A buzz distracted her left ear. Some time ago, she had decided that her father's ship had been lost at sea like so many others. All its passengers were drowned, tumbled to the ocean floor, where her father's body drifted still in blue-green water, rocked back and forth in salty current, the fish not daring to nibble his flesh, his flesh still firm and miraculously preserved.

How else could she explain why he had not come back for her?

But how could her father have written a book if he were drowned and dead on his way to Spain? How could the friar be talking of her father who lay under the sea?

Teresa dropped her rosemary and grabbed the monk's robe, nodding as if to say, "Take me now."

Fray Tomás looked startled. "Right now?" he asked.

Teresa nodded and pulled commandingly at his robe.

The Governor was not in his compound today. But the Governor's secretary, seemingly bemused, heard the friar's request. Yes, the girl could enter the library and see her former master's journal if the friar really wanted her to, if he had promised their guest, the brave and accomplished Álvar Núñez Cabeza de Vaca. Why not?

Teresa kept her eyes on the tiled floor and did not know if the secretary looked at her then, his eyebrows raised at her flattened head and tattooed cheeks. Hardly daring to breathe, she followed the monk down a strange hall she had never seen before. For the first time, she realized that there were many rooms in the Governor's house she had never seen, that she lived in a small world with just a few paths, from the kitchen to the stables, from the kitchen to the chapel, from the kitchen to the herb garden.

The library smelled of leather and lemon oil. Teresa stared at all the books on the shelves. They reminded her of clay pots, each holding some new food, perhaps a spice or unknown herb. Which one spoke in her father's voice? She watched the monk take down a bound manuscript and lay it precisely on an *escritorio*. With the tips of his fingers, he turned the pages and began to translate what the black lines and blotches meant. He started with the long introduction to the King, Charles the Fifth:

O Sacred, Holy, Imperial, Catholic Majesty! Among all the princes in the world, none approach your magnificence, the bright light of your wisdom and compassionate soul shining like a star in the early evening . . .

Immediately Teresa recognized her father in the words. There was no doubt. Her father was speaking to her again. When the friar stopped, she signaled him to read on. He looked at her with a crafty expression. "Will you speak to me now, Teresa?" the monk coaxed.

She signaled again, and he sighed and read.

Like the Italians with their feuds and labyrinthine strategies for war . . .

The Capoques are also a generous people.

We must meet them with kindness, as they have so often met me wandering lost in the wilderness . . .

At this passage, Fray Tomás looked up earnestly. "Your master agrees with the Franciscans, my order. He urges the King and all the Spanish kingdom to treat the Indians as if they have souls, to meet them with the love of Christ. This book has been very influential, Teresa. The King has decreed that some Indians can no longer be taken as slaves but should be given the rights of free men or, at least, of servants like yourself. Your master is a great man, Teresa. You should be proud to have traveled with him."

Teresa signaled again: read on. Her veins were on fire. Her head buzzed. Her father had written his report to the King of Spain in conversations with her. She had been the page on which he had inscribed himself, setting his life to memory as he lived it, always thinking of what he would say to Charles the Fifth and the royal court, always planning for the time when the Royal Treasurer of the Pánfilo de Narváez expedition would return to Seville.

Read on! She signaled to the friar.

The Mariames sometimes kill their female children at birth. The tribes inland can be cruel but often have great love for each other. It is noteworthy that these people take only one wife, except for medicine men, who may have more.

Where does he talk about me? Teresa wondered. Where am I in his book?

The women in the kitchen sang: *Sarampión toca la puerta. Viruela dice: ¿Quién es? Y Escarlatina contesta: ¡Aquí estamos los tres!* The cook would sometimes shout a little madly, "Sing it again!" And the women would sing again: Measles knocks at the door. Smallpox asks, Who's there? And Scarlet Fever replies: All three of us are here!

Everyone—the cook, the assistant cooks, the assistants to the assistants—felt it in the air. A bad time was coming. Every few years, New Spain seemed to experience such an epidemic. Sometimes it was measles, deadly to many adults and almost all babies. Sometimes it was smallpox, dreaded for the horrible days of pain with sores that began in the mouth and throat. Sometimes it was scarlet fever with its alternating chills and heat, or typhus, *tabardillo,* whose small red spots covered a woman like a *tabardo* or sleeveless cloak, growing closer and closer together over her chest and shoulders. Everyone in the kitchen had a story of a mother or sister or brother or daughter or son who had died of one disease or another, of entire families dying and villages left empty.

Teresa was not afraid. Teresa did not care. She was too angry. She was angry all the time now, and this anger filled her with unexpected power. Anger was a food better than bread, richer than chocolate. She had never known how good anger was, how it scalded and purified, tempered and strengthened. Every morning, she woke in a rage.

It began with Fray Tomás reading her father's journal on the beautifully decorated *escritorio*. He did not, of course, read about Teresa. In her father's story, in *the story*, Teresa did not exist. It began, perhaps, much earlier, on the beach in the hazy whiteness of the sea and sand and her father's words surrounding her before she could walk, before she could speak.

Fray Tomás noticed it right away. "Something is wrong with your heart, Teresa. It is growing hard."

She glared at him, refusing to go into the chapel, to sit meekly through one more sermon. The monk shook his head and pointed to the twisted heart carved into the wood of the chapel door. "Remember the bleeding heart of Christ, Teresa. It is a symbol of His fifth bleeding wound. He bleeds for you."

Teresa snorted.

The friar looked shocked. "Oh, yes!" Fray Tomás put a hand on his chest, on the rough brown cloth of his robe. "He loves you, and He cares for you." The friar hardly knew what to do, how to help this angry young woman.

Teresa snorted again when he tried to pat her head. Then she turned on her heel and walked away, leaving him with the other sleepy girls of the household in the light of another pink and yellow dawn.

The housekeeper was also puzzled. She had grown to depend on this tattooed child from the north who never wasted time gossiping or singing or giggling with her friends. There was always so much work to do, and with the rumors of sickness in Mexico City, some servants had started to run away. Now more than ever, the housekeeper needed willing hands in the kitchen to cut up meat and make tortillas and stir the soups. She needed calm faces and strong backs. She hardly recognized this new Teresa, who frowned at the slightest order and looked at her with contempt.

"What has happened to you?" the housekeeper exclaimed finally.

An assistant cook joined the conversation. "Fray Tomás says she has a hard heart. It happened overnight, he says."

"It is good to have a hard heart," another woman spoke. "Everyone knows that a bad temper is good protection against disease."

The housekeeper grumbled about turkeys that had to be plucked and dirty floors that had to be swept and the dozens of tortillas that had to be made before breakfast. Teresa noticed that the housekeeper's cheeks were flushed red, the pockmarks a bit more noticeable, the black eyes a bit too bright.

"Are you sure *you* are not sick?" the cook asked with a touch of malice.

"*Sarampión toca la puerta*," the assistant cook carelessly sang.

The housekeeper drew in her breath for everyone to hear and slapped the assistant cook across the face. "There is plenty of strength in these arms," she warned before she hurried from the kitchen.

The next day, she did not come down from her room.

That afternoon, the Governor left the house with a large group of men and a string of horses packed with supplies. His secretary informed the cook that the Governor would return in a few weeks, after his business was completed in the countryside. For now, the secretary was in charge, and the household work should continue as usual. Except there would be no more formal dinners. The secretary, himself, preferred to eat alone.

Two more servants became ill, and a few more ran away. Every morning, one of the assistants to the assistant cook came down to the kitchen to report that the housekeeper's fever was higher, her body like a stove. The housekeeper had also developed a rash that moved down her pockmarked skin from her hairline to her feet. Certainly she had the measles, the dreaded *sarampión*. The assistant to the assistant cook looked scared, although she did as she was told and went up again to put cold cloths on the housekeeper's forehead and to bring her water.

Finally she said that the housekeeper was dead, or almost so.

Teresa did not cry. She did not feel sad at the news. Soon the assistant to the assistant cook became sick, and then the assistant cook and then a third woman from the kitchen. Teresa helped take care of them because she knew she was safe from the disease. Because her hard heart protected her.

Fray Tomás was also busy tending the feverish children at his school. Whenever Teresa saw him, he looked terrible, his neck wrinkled and thin as a turkey's, his face hollowed and voice hoarse. As always, he seemed to be running even when he was not. As always, he asked about Teresa's health and happiness and gave her his blessing. He told her that the village of shopkeepers and blacksmiths and artisans was emptying quickly. Typically, they had eaten less well than the Governor's household and seemed more affected by the epidemic. Most of the slave hunters had departed with the Governor, and their Indian families had fled the area or were sick and dying unattended. Most of the children in the monk's care were orphans.

The Governor's secretary did not get sick, for he was a Spaniard, and they had special charms against all forms of disease, *sarampión* and *viruela*, *escarlatina* and *tabardillo*. The Spanish men left behind with the secretary also did not sicken but seemed dismayed and surprised at the deaths of their wives and sons and daughters. More and more they spent their time burying or burning the dead from the village. Soon that included the dead from the household: the assistant to the assistant cook who had tended the housekeeper, two assistant cooks, and two stable boys. Teresa had only to drag a body out to the court-yard, and it would disappear.

By this time, almost everyone else in the Governor's house had run away or was already fevered. Teresa did not know who was feeding or taking care of the Governor's secretary, or if he had already gone. She never saw him. She never saw anyone but the remaining Indian servants, who were all sick, and a few slave hunters and Fray Tomás. She understood now that she could do whatever she wanted to do. She could wander through all the rooms of the Governor's house alone. She could enter her father's bedroom and open again the wardrobe with its smell of sweet wood. She could go into the library and take down her father's book, although she could not read it. She could throw the book into the kitchen fire and watch it burn.

In fact she had no energy for these things since she spent most of the day bringing water to her demanding patients, pre-paring gruel for them, and washing and changing their bed-ding—the fine cotton cloths she used freely from the chests upstairs. One woman thanked her before she died. Another cursed her.

Fray Tomás stopped by the kitchen to get food. "You are doing good work," he praised. "You are a good girl, Teresa." He looked as though he were about to fall down.

Teresa shrugged. She wasn't trying to be good. She hadn't cared when the housekeeper died or any of the others. She simply took their bodies out to the courtyard.

"God bless you," the friar said as he picked up the basket of meat and tortillas and fruit. His blue eyes glittered too brightly. "They are all going to Heaven, you know. I have seen it myself. I have seen their souls slip up to the sky."

Teresa looked thoughtfully at the friar before she nodded. She had seen that, too. Pointing at the basket, she made the gesture for eating and then for sleeping. Pointing her finger at the friar, she shook it in a scolding way. He should eat more! He should sleep more! Fray Tomás shrugged apologetically. Probably she was right, but who had the time when so many people needed him? He trudged away.

That evening, her own fever surprised her. Teresa knew she wouldn't die, because of her hard heart, but the fever came anyway, and she went to her last two patients, changing their bed cloths one more time, leaving them water and a pot of soup. She touched the mottled skin on their faces. Both seemed cooler. She shook her head. She could only hope for the best.

Then she dragged herself from the kitchen to a pile of clean dry straw in the nearest barn. The horses were gone, taken by the Governor, although the stable still smelled pleasantly of old manure. The air was dark and cool, and before she collapsed, she also surrounded herself with pots of water and a covered pot of soup. There would be no one to put cold cloths on her forehead or moisten her lips or change the straw. She would be alone with her *sarampión*, just the two of them.

Teresa's head ached until she wanted to twist it from her neck as she would have twisted off the head of a chicken. Tossing and turning, burning and groaning, she saw wonderful things even as the sores appeared, first on her face, then moving like a feathery tip of fire to her chest and groin. Fire and feathers. She saw brushstrokes in the air from the wings of angels. She saw Juan Diego, the man who carried roses to the Bishop, his apron glowing with a picture of the Lady. She saw Fray Tomás, too, and this was not so wonderful, for the friar was bleeding from his mouth and nose and ears, from every opening in his body. She saw his soul, a yellow sheen, slip up into the sky.

She saw the wise woman. This was the most vivid dream of all. It was the old wise woman who lived with the coyote pup and the owl on the loudly talking, magic-filled hill, the wise woman who had kept the helmet from the conquistador and used it as a scarecrow in her field of maize. The woman's long braided hair was bone-white, her brown face creased into a web of wrinkles. Her eyes were dark. Her mouth had sunken. Around her neck, over wrinkled breasts, she wore a seashell necklace, pearl-white with gleams of coral pink.

The wise woman looked directly at Teresa. She did not look at Teresa's father. She was not interested in Teresa's father. "What you have lost will be restored to you," she said. With a painful leap of her hard heart, Teresa knew the wise woman was speaking to her and no one else.

Tossing and turning in the straw bed, Teresa reached out to the air, the brushstrokes of angels. She was thirsty. But she did not have the strength to find and lift a pot of water. Her skin itched, and she remembered all the women and men she had nursed and how they had scratched their bleeding sores and made them more inflamed. Like them, she couldn't resist. She itched and scratched.

What had she lost?

She had lost everything. She had lost her mother, cheerful and smiling. She had lost her grandfather, her uncles and aunts, her baby sister. She had lost her foster mother, who had tattooed Teresa's cheeks to make her a member of that tribe. She had lost the Moor, who had carried her when she was tired. She had lost her father, the deceiver. The betrayer. She had lost her soft human heart. She had lost the housekeeper with her powerful arms and stern pockmarked face. She had lost Fray Tomás.

What did the wise woman mean? Teresa reached out to the air.

What would be restored to her?

She knew when her fever broke, feeling it crack and fall away, freeing her arms and legs and loosening its hold on her chest. She crawled to where she had placed the closest clay pot, lifting the lid with a trembling hand and spilling the liquid over her face and shoulders and floor of the barn. Some of the coolness splashed deliciously on her lips and down her throat. Teresa gasped and breathed in the odor of straw, horses, and her own urine. The air smelled so good. She felt so good, despite her aching muscles, despite the rash that still dotted her neck and shoulders down to her stomach. She was weak. She was sticky with sweat and dirt. But she felt so good.

And she had something to do. She could still hear the wise woman's voice. She hadn't understood then, when she was a child. She hadn't realized that the wise woman had been talking to her and not her father. *What you have lost will be restored to you.* Now Teresa had to return to that village, back to that hill and crumbling adobe house. Now she had someplace to go.

6

A large raven flew into the barn and perched on an empty stall. *Kro-ak, kro-ak.* The bird rattled, weirdly liquid, and Teresa woke from her second sleep of the day. The raven turned its dark eye on her and croaked again before flapping with a dramatic flutter of wings outside into the summer sunshine. Teresa agreed. It was time. She was stronger now, having rested a full day and drunk her pot of soup and all her pots of water. She should stand now and go outside and find something more to eat.

She still wore her stained cotton shirt and leather skirt. She found her yucca sandals and staggered out the barn door, feeling the weakness of her legs as she followed the bird past the garden and into the courtyard. There she stopped, paused, and returned to the rooms by the kitchen where she had kept her last two patients. They were gone. Perhaps they had died and the Christians taken their bodies. Perhaps they had recovered and left on their own. She no longer had any responsibility here.

Unsteady, she walked into the village, where the dirt path was rutted and she had to be careful not to fall. She was thirsty again, and the light rash on her chest burned and itched. Just as Fray Tomás had said, the village was empty. Teresa looked about with interest, in part because she had been to the village so seldom, rarely leaving her kitchen and garden. The small adobe houses stood silently, surrounded by small yards of maize and beans, the ears ripening, the pods dangling unpicked from the vines. No one was in the blacksmith shop or the woodshop where the Indians had learned to make Spanish chairs, tables, and beds. The door to the whitewashed chapel was open, the twisted heart carved into wood. Here there was only more silence, and Teresa didn't stop to look inside.

But she paused before the building that had been the friar's school, wondering if there were any children who needed care and forcing herself to go in. Only Fray Tomás lay sprawled on the floor, one hand clutching his torn brown robe. From the black blood, Teresa knew the monk had been visited by *tabardillo,* a friend to *sarampión.* She was not surprised. She had seen this in her visions.

She hurried out of the foul-smelling room onto the dirt street, where the sky was turning darker blue and the shadows in the yards deepening. Ahead, a second raven perched on a post in front of an adobe house, its roof made of cane and woven leaves. The bird cawed, agitated. A Spanish man appeared in the doorway. He and Teresa stared at each other.

"Go on," the man said. "Get out of here."

The raven flew down the path, and Teresa followed. So a few people were still alive. They waited in their homes for the pestilence to pass. As she walked on, slowly, two more houses showed signs of life. In each case, a man came out and stared at her, afraid she had come because she was sick and needed help.

Teresa walked through the village, and then she left the village and the Governor's house and the Governor's kitchen behind her. She would never go back, never see them again. She was walking north along a well-worn path. She was searching for a stream where she could drink and wash herself and her clothes.

Soon she began to notice the animals. A large king snake, brown as chocolate, slithered in front of her flicking its tail.

This was the snake that ate other snakes, even rattlesnakes and the poisonous banded coral. A family of deer accompanied her for half a league, picking their way through the thorny brush where she could hear the brittle snapping of twigs. Sometimes they scrambled ahead so that she saw their rumps in a flash of white. Lizards darted across the trail, scurried here and there, here and there, here and there, and then watched her from a stone or root. Some had streaks of brilliant blue around their throat and bright orange on their belly. Birds flitted through the air like falling leaves, branch to branch, tree to tree, more birds than Teresa had ever seen before. She knew some of them from her hours in the Governor's garden: jays and gnatcatchers, wrens and robins, doves and finches. A flock of parrots flew like a green cloud in the darkening sky. Quail rustled in the grass.

As Teresa walked further into the summer night, she saw cuckoos and heard the whoooo of owls. Finally she found the stream she knew would be there, what the farmers used to irrigate their fields, and she drank and cleaned herself, scrubbing away the stains of sickness. Tired, she made a bed off the path, near the water. A wolf called another wolf in a valley beyond. From the ground, Teresa could feel the warmth of small mammals, mice and packrats, sleeping in burrows. Her stomach growled. The new abundance of animals seemed to answer back, growling and rustling. She went to sleep, and the animals ran through her dreams, winding like ribbons over her breasts and arms and legs, winding through her hair. She felt the stirring of her old life, when this had been normal, when the world had been alive in her body.

The next morning, she reached another village. Some of the houses smelled of rotting flesh, and she did not enter these. But one house had only the fragrance of pink roses planted as a hedge around the yard, and in this kitchen, she found food, her mouth watering at the sight of dried meal not yet eaten by mice, dried jerky in a sealed clay jar, and dried chilies hanging from a nail. She opened all the cupboards and filled a leather saddlebag also left behind.

Oh—she smiled when she found that bag, for it had a pocket that contained treasure. Teresa recognized the tinderbox immediately, small and wooden and carved with a simple floral design. Inside were a piece of flint, a curved piece of steel, and tiny pieces of prepared oilcloth. Now she could make a fire whenever she wanted.

This village and the one close by were completely abandoned. Not everyone had died. There weren't enough bodies. But the survivors had gone, leaving their dead just as Teresa had left hers in the Governor's courtyard. When the bodies in a house were old and dry enough, she went inside to look for more food. Most of the corpses lay on pallets and had their faces covered. Only a few had been left to die alone, without anyone or anything by their side.

Strangely confident, the animals wandered through the villages, too, as easily as they wandered through the forest. Teresa saw skunks and raccoons, coatis and opossum, rabbits and hares. Lying on the roof of one house, a mountain lion stretched out comfortably, eying her as she walked by. In the orchards of apples and pears and plums, in the fields of maize and beans and squash, pigs and cattle also roamed at their ease.

Occasionally she saw signs of people. In the dirt, there would be footprints, the litter from a recently eaten meal or the remains of a campfire. Once she heard voices in the distance, but she did not go toward them.

Outside the third village, the last adobe house smelled clean, the neatly swept dirt in the yard littered with fallen grass from the sagging roof. A tall yucca grew by the door, the spiky leaves at its base trailing threads that could be twisted into rope, the thick stalk rising up in an abundance of white flowers. Here, too, someone had planted pink and red roses, which bloomed in a fragrant mass of scent. Teresa stood and breathed in the perfume. She felt reassured. Beyond a corner of the house, blue sky showed with the brilliance of late afternoon, her second full day of traveling. Teresa adjusted the saddlebag slung across her shoulder. She wanted to scavenge quickly and be gone.

Inside the house, the first room contained nothing but broken pots smashed into pieces and scattered on the ground. In the second room, a back door let in a shaft of light in which the dust motes seemed to hold still like a solid thing in the air. Here Teresa caught that familiar odor, not of death but sickness, *cámaras de sangre* or bloody stools. Someone groaned along the wall, and a bundle of rags shifted before flinging itself into that solid shaft of dust and light. Teresa shrank back as a hand fell out of the bundle, then an arm, and the woman on the floor groaned again. Against her breast, she clutched a dead child.

Now a man's body blocked the back doorway. He spoke in Spanish, "What? What do you want?"

Teresa shook her head. She didn't want anything.

"You can't help her," the man said as he went to the woman and rearranged her limbs. Patiently he folded the dead child back into her arms. He turned and stared at Teresa, his eyes focused on something else. Suddenly he sounded angry. "I am taking care of her. Are you a priest?"

Still shaking her head, Teresa moved slowly to the open back door, ducked, and was out and walking fast past a ramada of ocotillo branches, long limbs of a spidery cactus with needle-sharp thorns and red flowers. At a wooden post, a horse stood with a bloody muzzle where the halter had cut his skin. The ground around the horse's hooves was pawed bare from his attempts to break free, but the rope tied to his halter and the post had knotted firm and held fast. As she rushed by, Teresa glanced over. She could count the animal's ribs.

Unexpectedly, the gelding spoke: help me.

Teresa was in a hurry to get away from the crazy Spanish slave hunter. But when the gelding's image and voice formed in her mind, she stood still. It had been a long time. She had stopped speaking and stopped listening, and the plants and animals had stopped speaking and listening to her, too. The world had gone silent. Still, now, she could hear this horse. Something had happened when she was sick and feverish. A bar on the door had fallen away. The door had opened a crack, and now the door was swinging wide.

Inside the house, the horse's master tended his sick wife and dead child. He had forgotten everything else. He had abandoned everything else. He had left his horse to die of thirst and hunger.

Help me, the gelding repeated. He loved me once. He cared for me.

The animal grieved for his master's sanity.

I need water! Suddenly the horse shied, spraying drops of blood and mucus, bursting to life. Untie me! Untie me now!

And Teresa did, as quickly as she could, although the rope had been pulled and tightened so fast to the post that her fingers were soon bruised. When the brown horse was finally free, he trotted off in another burst of energy, the rope trailing and jerking behind like a frenzied snake. Teresa knew the animal was rushing to the nearest stream outside the village. She followed him there, running for the first time in years, the saddlebag bouncing against her back.

After he had finished drinking, the gelding flared his nostrils and swung his head toward her, ears flattened. What do you want? the horse asked sullenly, echoing his master.

Teresa studied the well-proportioned body with its deep chest and long neck. What did she want? she asked herself. When she concentrated, she could catch more scattered images of the gelding's life. She could see the Spanish *hidalgo*,

66

outfitted in metal armor, so proud of himself and his handsome mount. They had been in battle together. They had killed men together. They had crossed the ocean together. Every night, the man rubbed the horse and gave him grain. He rubbed the long neck and whispered fond words.

The horse missed his master and ached to go back to him.

You can't go back, Teresa said—although not out loud. He won't even see you. He has forgotten you.

Yes, the horse agreed, still sullen. He is not my master anymore. He has become unhinged, crazed with grief and sorrow. In the grip of madness, he has betrayed his vows to himself and the captain he followed here for gold and silver, even as death has betrayed him.

Teresa blinked. The flavor of this animal's mind was distinct. She had not heard this kind of speech for some time. In the kitchen, they spoke less pompously. Even Fray Tomás had been a simple man of simple words.

I want you to take me north, she said. I have a long way to go, and it will take me weeks if I have to walk.

The horse shook his mane and rolled his eyes. Only my master rides me!

Teresa knew that tone, too. The pride, the arrogance.

Death has betrayed your master, she reminded the animal. He is not the same man. And I need you. I have a task for you.

You are a female, the horse protested. You are an Indian.

But he seemed unsure of himself.

How dare you? Teresa shrilled in return, trying to sound haughty. My great-grandfather was Pedro de Vera, the conqueror of the Grand Canary! My father was Cabeza de Vaca, treasurer of the Pánfilo de Narváez expedition! I come from a line of noblemen, *hidalgos,* and conquistadors.

The horse was impressed. But still reluctant.

I don't mean right away, Teresa said more kindly. You should graze first. You should rest first. I'll wait here, and then we will walk on together. We will go slowly as you regain your strength and calm.

Shaking his ears, the horse blew air through his nostrils and bent to pull at the sweet grass by the stream. Teresa moved away, breaking the connection between them. She wanted to think and plan alone. She coveted the gelding's deep chest and muscular legs. She coveted his ability to walk without tiring, twenty leagues a day. She felt the need to hurry, the wise woman calling to her, the wise woman who wanted to see her, who had something to tell her. *What you have lost will be restored to you.*

Teresa scratched at the remaining spots on her stomach. It would be easy enough for the horse to go wild in the orchards full of ripening fruit and fields full of ripening maize. She had to convince the animal now, while he was still tame.

She crept closer and stooped for the rope trailing in the grass.

What are you doing? the horse jerked.

Nothing, Teresa soothed. I am going to loop this over your neck and knot it so it doesn't catch on a bush. I am going to wet my cotton shirt, like this, and wash the cuts on your face.

And you will groom me later? the horse asked. He shivered, despite the heat.

I will make a comb out of sticks, Teresa promised. Eat now, and I will wash you, and I will groom you.

Huffing, confused, the horse dropped his head.

They walked on, the gelding moving slowly, still weak. When the first stars began to appear in the sky, Teresa found a place to camp, and that night she used the tinderbox, striking the flint hard against steel. The sparks caught in the tiny piece of oiled cloth and burned red. Quickly she put the cloth in a bird's nest with bits of her hair and blew—gentle puffs. Soon she had a fire to admire as she ate her dried jerky. The horse seemed used to the flames and came close as if to watch them, too. Teresa made a bed of grass for herself, while the horse said he would sleep standing up.

What should I call you? Teresa asked.

My master had a name for me, the horse flared. No one but he can use it. You can call me Horse.

That's fine, Teresa said.

You are not my master, the horse insisted.

I know, Teresa soothed him.

She wondered if she should tie the animal up for the night, if he would allow her to do that. She decided he would not. Not yet.

She lay down to sleep.

Did you hear that noise? Horse asked in a few moments, pricking his ears forward.

It's only a skunk, Teresa mumbled. There are so many animals now, everywhere.

I think this one is watching us, Horse whispered. This one has been following us.

Following us? Teresa tried to peer into the darkness, blacker against the light of the campfire. Suddenly she had the same feeling, as though it had been passed to her from the cautious animal. The horse ninnied, a sharp eerie sound. Teresa felt eyes on her skin. Yes, Horse was right. Someone was following them.

7

Teresa and the horse stayed awake, waiting, anticipating, while nothing happened, nothing at all. She fed the fire until it blazed high, yellow and orange flickering against the starry night. By the time the flames had died down again, her eyes were drooping. At last, they both slept, woke to the broad light of day, ate some food, and walked on. Teresa did not try to ride the horse, who was still weak and suspicious of her. Also she was a little scared. She had never ridden an animal before and wondered if she would fall off, the first time and every time.

They crossed a second stream, where yellow flowers bloomed along the bank. Big slow fish glided in a pool sheltered by the green leaves of cottonwoods, and Teresa thought of stopping to make a net of yucca rope—catching the trout, building another fire, roasting and eating the flaky white meat. Her appetite was returning, her fever completely gone, only sprinkles of rash on her thighs and stomach. Fish sounded good. A stew of rabbit meat and squash and beans sounded good. Wild duck sounded good.

The horse had already begun to graze. Teresa gave the gelding a few moments while she squatted by the water, one hand on her cheek, thinking of nets and traps. When she was small, she had seen the Indians of many different tribes make such things. It would take time and effort to learn to make them herself. But that's what she would do, she decided. She would make a net.

I'd like some grain, the horse said mournfully.

Of course, Teresa said. But I think we should avoid the villages for now.

She didn't say why. The horse already knew.

Someone might desire me, the gelding agreed, and not all masters are good ones. Most are not. I have seen great cruelty among those who follow their captains to war and conquest. I have seen men beat their mounts until the blood ran. I have seen men take their weapons and hack each other to death for the metal they carry in their pockets or the chance to become more powerful and wear clothes of a different color.

What else have you seen? Teresa asked, interested. She flicked a pebble into the water, watching to see if a fish would rise.

Horse raised his head instead of answering. Teresa's skin prickled, too. They were still being followed. Something watched them from the bushes by that line of trees, something clever and patient. It would be gone by the time she ran to beat through the thorny branches. Even now, it was creeping away.

What could they do but walk on?

It's a wolf, Teresa guessed.

No, Horse said. I don't smell wolf.

Later in the day, to pass the time, he told her about his life in Spain—how he had been born in a stable in the city of Granada. His mother also had been a mercenary's horse, and from the start, her colt was meant to be the same. His master had trained him with gentle firmness, and while they were both young, they had gone to fight in a place where the people spoke strangely and smelled bad.

The Italian wars, Teresa thought. *Like the Italians with their feuds and labyrinthine strategies . . .*

When they returned to Granada, the horse and his master had a few glorious months of resting and eating before all the money was spent on grain and apples, gambling and women. Then there was nothing to do but sign up for another war or expedition. This time, his master chose a ship bound for the New World.

The stories were familiar to Teresa, although told from a different view. The horse remembered stables, not churches, and silver bridles, not inlaid writing desks. He didn't groan about fruit tarts and meat pastries but oats sweetened with honey and apricots from a tree in his master's garden. Still, it was the same Spain that Teresa had heard so much about as a child: the fine clothes and dramatic processions in the cobbled streets, the smell of incense and baking bread, the burning of heretics and unbelievers.

After the horse and his master had crossed the ocean—and that was a miserable voyage, the horse said—they had to pass through Mexico City, the former capital of the proud and ferocious Aztecs. The horse's master had chattered with excitement. Clearly this town had once rivaled the great cities of Spain, as grand as Granada or Seville, and both horse and master marveled at the winding streets and buildings rising into the sky. Of course, many temples and public houses had been destroyed when the famously lucky Hernán Cortés and his five hundred men had conquered the Aztecs with the help of many thousands of Indian allies, the help of *sarampión* and *viruela*. But new churches and mansions were being built every day using the labor of slaves. As the horse had neared the center of town, the marketplace could be heard a league off, a roar of people shouting and selling meat, vegetables, herbs, dyes, cloth, silver, gold, parrots, and the prized blue and green quetzal feather.

The horse knew some good gossip, too, for the New World was a small world for Spanish *hidalgos,* and everyone talked about each other's affairs. He had heard, for example, what had happened to the Moor, the man Teresa's father had called Esteban, who had been sold to the Governor to lead an expedition north. The expedition's task was to discover the Seven Cities of Gold. As always, the Moor was the one who went on ahead, talking to the tribes and shaking his painted gourds. The story went that his claims became more and more extravagant until finally, in one village, he told the Indians that he was a god as well as a healer. Properly impressed, his hosts tested his divinity by cutting him up and eating the pieces. The Moor died bloodily, and the rest of the expedition scurried home with their tails between their legs. Even so, Horse said, the Governor still believed that the north was full of villages with streets paved of gold. Even so, the Spanish dreamed of extraordinary wealth, riches beyond imagination.

Teresa listened but felt nothing. Her hard heart protected her. Casually, she found herself asking: have you heard of a man called Andrés Dorantes?

Naturally, of course, Horse said. Dorantes and his famous companion Cabeza de Vaca had been lost in the most heathen wilds of the New World for eight years and then rescued by the Governor himself. Later the men had taken separate ships home to Spain, and Dorantes's vessel had proved unseaworthy. Limping back to Vera Cruz, he had been sent off by the Viceroy of Mexico City to subdue the Indians in the province of Jalisco. There he married a rich Spanish widow with whom he had three sons.

And Alonso del Castillo? Teresa wondered idly.

Another companion of the famous and celebrated Cabeza de Vaca, Castillo also did not go to Spain but only accompanied his friends to Vera Cruz in order to see them finally gone. He, too, had married a rich Spanish widow and was given half the Indian rents in a small southern town. No one heard much news from him, for he led a dour and solitary life. People said he was very religious.

And Cabeza de Vaca? Teresa finally murmured. What news of her father?

Like everyone who was anyone, the horse's master had discussed the conquistador who had written a famous book as a report to the King of Spain. Her father was a refined and ambitious gentleman with an influential wife. On her husband's return from his adventures in the most heathen wild, this influential wife had convinced the King to name Cabeza de Vaca as Governor of the Río de la Plata from Peru to the Straits of Magellan. With that title, he had sailed again from Spain to the New World. At the capital of his province, he pacified the Indians, forbade their slavery, defended their rights, and angered the Spanish colonists. Rumors now hinted that these colonists, as well as his own men, were rebelling against him. The horse snorted at the thought. His master had taught him better than that.

But Teresa was only mildly interested. Her hard heart whispered: so her father had returned to the New World. And the *sarampión*? she asked. How far does the epidemic spread?

The horse did not know since this was more recent news, after his master had gone sorrowfully mad with grief. I can tell you about other epidemics, the animal offered. I have seen smallpox sweep through Mexico City, killing thousands and burning and disfiguring everyone it touched. Only the Spanish escaped, especially those already pocked.

Go on, Teresa agreed, happy to keep him talking as they walked along the trail.

They skirted two villages that day, and she felt more strongly that this was the right thing to do. She remembered the Moor although she did not grieve for him, and she felt disgust at the way they had once traveled, entering and leaving village after village with the large crowds streaming behind. So many people. So much noise, clapping and shouting. Her father had made speeches. He had made the sign of the Cross and the man or woman jumped up healed. She remembered how the Opata children would run toward the healers in anticipation.

She remembered the sound the people had made when the Spanish slavers took their baskets of food and ringed them with horses. This was not the kind of journey she would ever make again.

Soon she would make a net, Teresa thought. She would learn again to gather berries and the roots of plants, how to trap small animals and hunt bigger game. For now, there were also the abandoned fields of maize, squash, and beans. There were orchards of hard green fruit—not yet good to eat. But soon.

At one of these orchards, they stopped so that the horse could graze. Let's stay the night, he said lazily.

We have hours of daylight, Teresa protested.

But I like this grass, Horse insisted.

He nudged her shoulder as if begging, and Teresa was pleased. Already, the horse needed her approval. Very well, she replied. Privately, she thought: tomorrow I will ride you. Tomorrow we will travel far to the north.

While the horse rested, Teresa experimented with getting fresh meat for her own meal. She waited in a good spot until a young rabbit emerged from its burrow, and then she dropped it with a stone. Surprised at this easy success, and while the animal was still stunned, she slit its throat using a knife she had found in the last village. Triumphant, she did this again when a second young rabbit hopped from the burrow although she knew she could not eat two for supper.

She hung the second one from a tree near their campfire.

The attack came when they were both asleep. This was not supposed to happen, for they had agreed they would take turns on guard, something the horse had learned from his master and the master's captain. To Teresa's chagrin, she was the one who drifted off, closing her eyes just when dawn was close and the pull of dreams strongest.

The horse squealed, high-pitched, and Teresa woke, jumped up, and grabbed a stick from the fire they had kept alive all night. A blur of movement nearby! A low deep growl! And the horse lifting his front legs in defense, striking out with his hooves.

The blur of movement moved away from the horse, closer to Teresa. Instinctively, she waved her stick, which flared newly orange. In the light, she saw the rabbit dangling. She saw the shine of green and yellow eyes, the jaguar's yellow-white fur also gleaming in the glow of the fire stick, which illumined a pattern of black spots. Teresa had seen the skin of a jaguar in the Governor's hallway—and earlier, too, in the wise woman's house—and she knew how the animal would look in the day: a beautiful gold fur covered with rings and circles of black. She stared entranced at the large rounded head, the small ears and powerful jaw.

The jaguar dropped the rabbit and grunted. *Hunh! Hunh!*

His back legs tensed. He would not attack the horse, who pawed at the air with hooves that could break ribs and crush a spine. But he was ready to spring at Teresa, launching himself against her chest and biting her neck.

He grunted again. *Hunh! Hunh!*

No, Teresa cried. Stop!

The jaguar froze.

Don't hurt me, Teresa babbled. You can have the rabbit. Leave us alone.

No words, no image came from the animal. But Teresa could feel its shock. The green-yellow eyes blazed and seemed to get bigger, bigger, brighter, and then dimmer.

Dimmer. And then they were gone. The jaguar was gone.

Teresa waved her stick, which flared anew.

A small boy lay on the ground.

8

The horse backed away, ears pointed forward at the child. Horse seemed as amazed as Teresa, and his hooves danced on the grass and dirt, ready to lash out if necessary. Teresa sat down, the ashes of the campfire blowing around her.

After a while, she realized she should do something for the boy, who had been gasping and crying for some time now. Standing and coming closer in the gray light of dawn, she saw that the child's eyes were closed and he seemed half-conscious. His face scrunched in anguished weeping. His fists knotted at his chest as he lay curled on the ground, no danger to anyone, helpless as a baby. His dark hair was fine, cut short at the ears. He was, Teresa guessed, four or five years old.

She touched him cautiously. The boy moaned. She shook his shoulders, trying to wake him, ready to spring back if he should turn into a jaguar again. But he only curled more tightly into a ball, moving his head against his thighs. Now Teresa tried to lift the child, hoping to break through his dazed sleep. He was heavier than she thought, and he still did not wake although he struggled, thrashing and flailing his arms and legs. She dragged him onto her bed of grass and then moved away to a safe distance.

From that place, she watched and waited as the sky brightened into shades of blue with a low wispy fog over the maize fields, a color like the inside of certain shells, luminous and pearl-white. Eventually the boy stopped making crying noises and slept more deeply, his long lashes dark against his cheek.

What is he? Teresa asked the horse, who watched with her.

I don't know. I have heard . . . Horse hesitated and then continued in a defensive tone as if afraid she would not believe him: I have heard of tribes in the south who have medicine men who can turn into animals. I have heard of shape-shifters, always from the south, jaguar-men. But I never believed those stories.

You never saw anything like this before? You never met anyone?

Not me, the horse nickered. My master did, someone who saw a Mayan slave . . . The animal bent his head, hungry, unsettled, torn between talking and grazing.

Go on, Teresa prompted.

My master had a friend who said he speared a Mayan slave just as she was turning into an animal. She died and became human again. But my master didn't believe him either. How can an animal also be a human? How can a human also be an animal?

The horse tore at the grass and refused to speak again. Teresa watched the little boy as the birds began their morning chorus, all together in a burst of chatter and call and musical sound, and as the sun rose higher, burning away the fog. She retrieved the rabbit from the ground, skinned and skewered the body, and built up a fire to roast her breakfast. Briefly she left the child to get water from the nearby stream, where she drank and filled a gourd. When she let some of its contents dribble into the boy's mouth, he sputtered and swallowed, sputtered and swallowed, and still did not wake. Not even the smell of cooking meat roused him.

Teresa studied the boy—the clear brown skin, flat nose, full lips, and dark lashes on a rounded cheek. He did not look sick or starved. But he did look uncomfortable, his face twitching and his hands clenched into fists. Occasionally he sighed or grimaced. He did not seem happy to be in his human skin. He did not even look fully human.

Or maybe it was only that Teresa had never spent much time with children. She had never played with other girls and boys, not since leaving her baby sister. She had spent her childhood traveling with her father and three other men, and then she had begun her work in the Governor's kitchen under the eye of the cook and assistant cook and assistants to the assistant cook. No one had thought of her as a child there or treated her like one. No one brought babies or children into the kitchen, for the housekeeper would not allow it.

Teresa picked at the meat on the rabbit bones. She felt nervous. It was mid-morning, past time to go. Today she was going to ride the horse. Today they would travel many leagues. The need to hurry built like a pressure in her chest. She needed to find the wise woman. The wise woman wanted her, waited for her.

Perhaps she and the horse should simply leave the boy here. She would give him the rest of the rabbit. There was water nearby. He could always hunt his own food. Perhaps that was for the best.

The horse came and nudged her from behind. Leave him here, the gelding advised. That's for the best.

He's too young, Teresa heard herself argue back. He can't take care of himself.

He was doing fine last night, Horse said.

But something is wrong now, Teresa worried. He's not waking up.

I don't like his smell, the horse complained. I don't like jaguars.

They waited all that day. Sometimes the boy roused enough to drink a little water or the soup Teresa made and kept warm.

Even then, he never opened his eyes and only muttered gibberish she could not understand. Sometimes she caught Spanish-sounding words. Sometimes he rambled in another language, perhaps Mayan, a tongue from the south. That night, she and the horse took turns resting and keeping guard. This time, she did not fall asleep.

The next morning, when the boy opened his eyes and spoke, it was only to scream loudly for his mother. "Mamá, Mamá, Mamá!"

"Be quiet," Teresa tried to shush him. Her voice came out rusty and strange, hardly intelligible. Drawing back, she realized this was the first time she had spoken out loud in eight years, since her father had left her in the courtyard of the Governor's house, since the turtle had kept moving across the sky and the world did not end.

The boy shrieked more vehemently. He wanted his Mamá! He wanted to go home!

"Where is your home?" Teresa tried asking. She wanted to slap him. She wondered if that would help or make things worse.

"Mamá! Mamá!" the boy yelled, a stream of tears welling up in his eyes and running down his cheeks. His nose streamed with a flow of mucus. "Mamá!" He drummed his hands on the ground and kicked his feet. "Mamá!" His back arched in a tantrum he seemed unable to control, as if a Bad Spirit were shaking him from the inside.

Teresa watched, appalled. The horse grazed.

The boy began weeping all over again. How could such a small body hold so much water? He cried, awake now, until he couldn't cry anymore, until he and Teresa were both exhausted. At some point, she had taken him onto her lap. She was stroking his hair, saying "Shush, shush" over and over. His dark head burrowed into her breasts, and he fitted himself against her stomach. "It's all right," Teresa promised, not knowing why but believing it herself at the moment. "It's all right. You're all right now."

"Ma . . . a . . . ma," the boy whispered and began to hiccup. Hic, hic, hic. The jerky movement of his body looked painful. Hic, hic, hic.

"Make it stop," he said plaintively in Spanish.

The horse had come close again, breathing down Teresa's neck.

Teresa was at a loss. How did anyone stop the hiccups? She jiggled the boy tentatively. "Giddy-up," she said. "Giddy-up, giddy-up." She bounced the child up and down on her lap. He coughed, whimpered, and sighed, the saddest sound Teresa had ever heard. His fingers gripped her breasts too tightly.

You did not groom me today, the horse said.

The sun shone pleasantly in the blue sky. Soon, Teresa thought, it would get too hot and they would need to move into the shade. "Giddy-up," she whispered with her new rough voice into the boy's ear. "Imagine you are riding a bay mare. You are on your way to a wonderful fiesta."

"A fiesta?" the child repeated. Hic, hic, hic. His chest heaved.

"A fiesta with wonderful food," Teresa promised.

"I'm hungry," the boy said. "I want some, hic, food!"

9

Teresa called him Boy although she knew he must have his own name, a Mayan one, at least, given to him by his mother and father. But Boy seemed easiest for now, and the boy seemed to agree. He didn't want to talk about the past. He gnawed ferociously on the leftover rabbit bones and then wanted something more. Teresa searched through her saddlebag and found a remaining slender squash that she had gathered earlier from a field.

The child made a face. "I like meat."

"I can see that," Teresa said. "Try this, and we'll get more meat, too."

Could the boy control his change into the jaguar, she wondered, or did that happen without warning? Did it happen when he was hungry?

Now the boy took such small bites of the vegetable that he looked like a mouse, nibbling delicately, his nose wrinkling with distaste. His teeth were white and strong, bigger, perhaps, than other children's teeth.

"Do you like fish?" Teresa asked, trying not to smile. She knew he would.

She cut away the rope halter from the gelding's muzzle. Then she unbraided the rope and made a misshapen and rough net, which she hoped would hold a trout for long enough to throw it on the bank. She and the boy walked down to pools that looked promising and got lucky at the second hole, where a fish drowsed unwary in the shadows. Teresa scooped it up as the tail flapped, and the trout almost slipped away until the net caught its nose again. Shouting with excitement, Teresa threw the entire thing into the air, and then the fish was in a bush, still flapping. The boy ran to club it with a rock.

"Good!" Teresa praised.

The boy danced, stomping his feet and lifting his chubby arms. With his chest puffed out, he grinned down at the fish. "We caught you," he said, and that was so obvious that Teresa almost smiled again.

It took much longer to catch a second fish. The net broke. The boy got bored and began to play a game in which he thrashed the yellow flowers on the bank with a stick, knocking off their petals and yelling in Spanish, "Get to work! Get to work!"

He must have seen such *hidalgos* and slave hunters, Teresa thought, in the place where he had lived before, perhaps in the silver mines or a garrison at some Spanish outpost. She doubted his parents had been slaves themselves in these mines. The child seemed too healthy, without scars and without a brand. More likely, they had been servants like herself, working in the kitchen, where there was lots of extra food. How had they managed to keep the boy's secret? Was his mother a jaguar-woman, too, and his father a jaguar-man, shape-shifters and shamans? And where were those parents now? Were they still alive? Teresa suspected not. She didn't think a mother would willingly leave a child so young and foolish and inexperienced.

"Be quiet," she ordered, without much success. At first, the boy would stop, and then in a few minutes, he would be bored again and thrashing flowers and yelling and dancing.

"This is not good for hunting," Teresa grumbled. "Come here now. Help me with this." She listened critically to her words. Yes, she still sounded rusty, her throat muscles stiff, her mouth awkward. Even so, the child understood and came to squat beside her. With two hands, she reached into a dark place where water had eroded the root-tangled bank. When she felt the ridged back of something slimy, she let the broken net spread, entangling the fish. The boy leaned over to see better, his hair brushing her cheek.

Suddenly, too close to her ear, Teresa heard a shriek and then water was in her nose. The boy had fallen in! He wailed and splashed, but Teresa kept her balance and kept hold of the fish, knowing that the pool wasn't very deep. The fish sailed up and plopped a good distance away on the dirt. Satisfied, she jumped into the water and grabbed the boy and held him up so he wouldn't drown. Then, without thinking, she made him laugh by tickling his stomach. His lips stretched wide and his dark eyes crinkled, and this made Teresa laugh back and soon they were both laughing and splashing so much that all the fish here were well warned and hidden. Teresa didn't mind. They could always walk farther down the stream. They could always find another pool.

She couldn't remember when she had laughed like this before. Of course, the cooks and the assistant cooks had laughed in the kitchen, telling jokes about the balding Fray Tomás and sometimes, more quietly, about the housekeeper. She had also seen girls giggling at chapel, whispering and poking when they should have been quiet. Once she had heard the housekeeper laugh genuinely at a handsome male gardener clowning for an extra pastry. And Fray Tomás often chuckled at something he said to himself or to his God or that his God said to him.

The memories sobered her, and she made the boy get out of the water, returning to the campfire with two fish to eat and two to save for later in the day. Teresa cooked these until the skins were burnt and wrapped them in wet leaves. Then she filled the leather bag with watercress. It was already afternoon.

She was ready to continue the journey north to find the wise woman.

But Horse wouldn't let the boy ride him. Never, the horse said. That's how jaguars do it. They jump on a horse's back, rake his flesh, and bite his neck. It doesn't take long. You bleed to death. Hell on your back! Ridden by the Devil! Your cries of agony resound in your ears.

Teresa could only suppose that the horse's master had talked like this, too.

No, she said firmly. I don't think so. He is not going to turn back into a jaguar. He is human now. Aren't you? she turned to the boy and asked. The child only stared and said nothing, so that Teresa understood the boy was like her father and the housekeeper and Fray Tomás and everyone else. He couldn't hear them speaking, horse to human, human to horse.

Never, Horse repeated. I was raised in the sweet perfume of the sweetest city in Spain. I have fought in foreign wars and sailed across the sea and slept in the stable of the Viceroy of Mexico City. I don't carry Mayan slaves.

For emphasis, the horse moved forward, reached out, and nipped the boy on the upper arm. The boy screamed. Horse! Teresa was shocked. The horse neighed and trounced away. The boy kept screaming until his soft chocolate-brown face turned purple. The skin on his arm had been broken, and a few drops of blood slid to the ground. But when Teresa tried to look at the bite, the child gnashed his teeth, and she jumped back.

"Ma . . . Ma! Ma . . . Ma! Mamá!"

So they were back to that.

Horse chuckled.

Teresa wondered how everything had slipped so quickly out of control.

When the boy calmed down—and that took some time—the horse agreed to walk beside them as they continued north. He would not carry them. He would only accompany them. Teresa felt tired in a different way from the tiredness of chopping vegetables and making tortillas and sweeping floors all day. Life was much easier when you lived alone and had no one but yourself. That's how it had been in the Governor's kitchen. Surrounded by people, she had still been alone, blessedly alone, never having to soothe and argue, pet and cajole, talk and convince.

Slowly, slowly, slowly, they followed the path to the next village as the boy ambled along on his short legs. Climbing a bit higher, they left the fields and orchards behind, with stunted pine trees now lining the way, mixed with oak and needled juniper. Teresa thought that she would never reach the wise woman at this rate. She was worse off now than before she had met Horse.

The yellowing sun had begun to drop and they only had a few hours more of light, when she felt eyes again on her skin and sensed an intelligence watching her from the branches of a rough-barked tree. She stopped, swiveled, and stared.

Horse felt it, too. He was also surprised. So it wasn't the jaguar-boy, he said.

"What do you want? Get out of here!" Teresa called out. The tangle of scrub oak and grass and juniper revealed nothing. They were the only three travelers on the path that stretched before and behind them.

Teresa tried again. "Who are you? What do you want?" But whoever had found them did not want to be found.

Let's go, Teresa said to the horse. "We have to hurry!" she scolded the boy.

Now the horse went ahead because he could smell water and scent out their next campsite. The boy walked in the middle, a prudent distance from the horse's back hooves, and Teresa brought up the rear, her skin crawling and senses alert. When they passed a fork in the trail, the horse wanted to take it to the valley below with its village and fields. But Teresa told him to keep climbing on the path that took them north, and soon they came to a spring edged with green grass and small blue flowers. As she and the boy ate a supper of wrapped fish, the horse grazed. No one spoke much. Without further discussion, she and the horse took turns guarding the fire.

The next morning, they started out again, climbing again, the way steeper now as it angled up the mountain slope. Almost immediately, the boy complained that his legs were tired. Teresa said his legs couldn't be tired so soon. They were barely out of camp. But the boy said his legs *were* tired, very tired, and he couldn't walk another step.

The horse stopped. What? Teresa snapped. Then she also felt eyes—the watcher, the person or animal or thing. She also turned to study the trees behind them, the space between bushes. It's still here, Horse said.

Yes, it's even closer.

The horse's ears went back.

The boy whined, "I don't want to walk!"

Teresa stared down the path. A black thread of smoke curled through a pine tree. Do you see that? she asked the horse.

It's our campfire, the horse said. The smoke uncurled until it rose up into a straight line, a thin black column. The column began to widen, thicker and thicker, filling the path like a solid wall. The solid wall began to move.

Now they both understood. The wall of black was *fear*, and *fear* was moving toward them on the path, gathering speed.

Teresa couldn't help herself. She whimpered. The horse squealed and shied, striking out with his hooves, just missing the boy's head. Terror exploded in Teresa's chest, paralyzing, then galvanizing her. She grabbed the horse's brown mane. Take us away! she pleaded. You have to take us away! Even as she spoke, she was reaching with one hand to pick up the boy and throw him onto the horse's back.

The horse startled and trembled. But his master had taught him this, too: you didn't leave your comrades behind. If your master was wounded, you waited for him to mount you. If there were wounded or horseless men on the field, your master waited and helped them mount.

Yes, Horse snorted, eyes a half-moon of white. Hurry!

Teresa slung the boy, who was crying and yelling, and then pulled herself up—she didn't know how. The leather bag bounced hard against her shoulder. She gripped the horse with her knees and entwined her fingers in his mane and flattened her body to cover the child and hold him to the horse. Go, go! she commanded, and the horse turned clumsily, trying not to dislodge her. He lifted his muscled legs and breathed in and ran up the path, away from the wall of *fear*.

Teresa concentrated on not falling, on not letting the boy fall.

10

They climbed until the path flattened and the horse could breathe more easily. Now he settled into a steady gallop, four beats, four beats, four beats, four beats, thud, thud, thud, thud. Teresa didn't need to look back. She could feel the black wall of *fear* behind them moving as fast as they but no faster. What was it? A Bad Spirit? A demon?

That is what Fray Tomás would say—that this was a fiend from Hell. But why was it chasing them?

Down the path they galloped, with Teresa's knees frozen, locked into place. The boy had stopped whimpering. He also gripped the horse's mane. Finally, after what seemed a long frightening time, the horse had to slow down, and the beat under them changed into a trot, two beats, two beats, thud, thud. Teresa could see. the blurred shapes of trees and bushes as they trotted by them. She had never traveled so quickly in her life, and under other circumstances she would have been pleased. She was riding Horse just like she had planned. She was riding a horse, just like her father, like the stories he had told her when she was small. She could feel the animal's muscles working under her. She was Horse's second half, part of his power.

Behind them, *fear* slowed, too, as if the black wall of smoke were also growing tired. Teresa dared to turn her head and look. The horse was faster than whatever followed them. They were pulling ahead.

Now they trotted through the narrow streets of a village with houses on either side. The horse slowed even more, almost to a walk. At first, this village also seemed to be empty, desolated by *sarampión*, its gardens overgrown. But when Teresa looked more closely she saw that the houses were not really abandoned. A man came to a doorway and peered at them. Then Teresa saw a woman walking the street and carrying a basket on her head. Somehow she had survived the disease. Moving out of their way, the woman stared. It wasn't the horse that surprised her. "A child," she exclaimed. Another man appeared at her side and also stared at the boy. "It's a child," he said in the same tone.

The village made Teresa nervous, as a second man came out of his house. She knew what had happened. All the children here had died. Let's go, she urged the horse, and he changed his pace to a canter, three beats, three beats, three beats, thud, thud, thud.

They ran and walked for hours more. Sometimes *fear* was close enough to see, and sometimes not. By afternoon, the horse was exhausted and had to drink. Stumbling, shambling, he went off the path toward a stream that Teresa knew was the same stream—farther north and bigger here—that they had stayed by yesterday, its waters rushing to the sea, its movement a kind of magic. It was the same stream where she had laughed and splashed with the boy a lifetime ago, before the wall of *fear*.

As she tumbled from the horse's back, Teresa cried out with pain. Her legs wouldn't straighten, and she could barely stand. On the ground, the boy also wept with the stiffness in his legs and buttocks.

I can't get back on, Teresa told the horse.

And I can't carry you further, Horse said. I have to stop.

Then we stay here, Teresa agreed. She staggered to the boy, half-falling, and stood in front of him, between him and the

Bad Spirit or the demon or the witchcraft or whatever this was.

But *fear* was gone.

Neither she nor the horse could feel it any longer. Locusts buzzed in the low twisted pine trees, crickets kept a steady chirping, a few birds called and scolded. The air was filled with the sounds of the forest. Teresa listened. Horse listened. Nothing followed. Nothing was behind them.

"I'll go look on the path," Teresa said out loud.

"Don't leave me!" the boy cried from the ground.

"Stupid. I'm not leaving you," Teresa reassured him.

She hobbled back the way they had come, the muscles in her legs protesting every step. Bravely, she looked up and down the trail. It was just a path that people used to walk from one village to the next. Animals used it, too, coyotes and deer, skunks and peccary and mountain lions, even the rare jaguar, trotting here and there on important errands. There was no wall of smoke, no blackness, no curling shadow. The trail, the day, the tracks in the dirt were perfectly ordinary. Soon it would be evening, and she should collect firewood. She should find something for them to eat.

Had it all been their imagination? Teresa tried to think so.

But the next morning, *fear* returned. It waited until the horse had grazed and Teresa and the boy had eaten their breakfast of wild onion and hard currants. It waited until they were back on the path, walking beside the horse, with Teresa still wondering if their pursuer was real.

And then *fear* was there. The horse and boy turned, staring behind them. The panic blossomed in their hearts, just as before, just as strong as before. They had to get away! They had to run! Once again Teresa and the boy threw themselves onto the horse's back, pulling at his mane, fumbling and gasping. This time, Teresa dropped the leather saddlebag that held the food and fishing net, the knife and gourd for water. There was no time to pick it up. At least she had knotted the tinderbox, her most prized possession, into her cotton shirt.

Go! she told the horse. And *fear* chased them all that day, down the path, leaving again by late afternoon and returning again the next morning.

In the next few days, they discovered that if they kept moving forward as quickly as they could without becoming exhausted, then *fear* would not come too close. Horse began to pace himself, walking briskly most of the morning and afternoon but no longer galloping uphill or down. They rose, ate breakfast, and continued their journey, Teresa and the boy on Horse's back. They stopped, ate lunch, and traveled again. In the remaining hours, Teresa gathered food, hunting at dusk when the young rabbits came out of their burrows. To skin and gut the animals, she used a rock that she chipped and sharpened until it resembled somewhat the knife they had lost. The path followed the stream, and along its edge she could also gather onions and berries and watercress. Now she had no saddlebag to store them in, and more than once, she scolded herself for leaving it behind.

Teresa remembered her journey with her father and the hares the hunters had harried from one man to the next. The men had made a sport of it, chasing an animal from bush to bush until the creature ran straight into a hunter's hand. In the same way, Teresa and Horse and Boy were being chased and teased from campsite to campsite, bush to bush.

They experimented.

If Teresa and the boy did not mount the horse but walked beside him, traveling more slowly than they would otherwise, *fear* began to gather on the path, sending out curls of black smoke and forming a solid wall. *Fear* invaded their minds. *Fear* seemed to fill the dark spaces of the forest. Eventually, the horse would roll his eyes so that the whites showed, and the boy would start crying, and Teresa would be fumbling at the horse's mane, throwing the boy up and pulling herself awkwardly onto the bony back.

Sometimes they tried leaving later in the morning or napping longer during their rest at lunch or ending earlier in the day. Then *fear* would gather, too, and they would ride on, traveling a few more leagues down the path.

Teresa's legs and rump were constantly sore now. She had never dreamed riding a horse could be so painful. Horse assured her that her body would eventually adjust to his, and she muttered back: couldn't it be the other way around? The boy suffered less, lying forward on his stomach and occasionally dropping his head to nap on the gelding's neck. Each time, Teresa kept him from falling, her knees locked, her arms stretched out at an awkward angle.

Strangely, though, Horse stopped complaining. He almost seemed to enjoy the regime of walking, grazing, walking, and grazing. This was, after all, what he had been trained to do. More than once, he commented that Teresa and the boy weighed far less than his helmeted, shielded, and armored master.

They did not enter any more villages. When they met other people on the trail, Teresa could see that the *sarampión* was still close by, for these men and women were cautious. Well dressed in leather skirts, their breasts painted with designs of red and white, they kept a good distance from the horse and his two passengers. Perhaps they were afraid of illness or perhaps they were like most Indians in New Spain, suspicious of horses and the ones who rode them. Sometimes a woman or man pointed at the boy, and sometimes they averted their eyes.

Now Teresa was traveling exactly as she had wanted to travel, fast and north, closer every day to the wise woman. She was glad of that, at least. The horse's "Never" had changed into a grudging acceptance. He was a horse. She was his rider. Patient at first, and then less so, the gelding tried to teach her tricks such as how to shift her weight to his different beats, the trot and the canter, how to mount and dismount gracefully. Teresa followed his instructions as best she could even as she grimaced with the ache of sore muscles and chafed skin. Horse commented on her efforts critically. Clearly she was not born to this skill.

The boy also seemed to accept the situation and regained a bit of good humor whenever they stopped and ate lunch or camped for the evening. He still liked to play with a stick, swishing off the heads of yellow flowers. He liked to make dams in the stream, where he caught water beetles and minnows, pretending these creatures were Spanish slave hunters and he was their captain giving them orders—to sleep, to eat, to ride out for the day. Then he would release the fish and insects from the dam and scramble to catch them again, splashing in the water, yelling furiously for them to come back.

Can't you keep him quiet? Horse muttered more than once. He's louder than cannon. The horse still didn't like the boy. He smells of jaguar, the horse said.

Meanwhile, the boy remembered the bite on his arm. "He's a bad horse," the boy told her solemnly as they drank one evening from the rippling stream. "He should be shot."

"No, no," Teresa hushed and looked about. Had Horse overheard? "He's a good horse! What would we do without him? How would we get away from . . ." She didn't finish the sentence. "He's a good horse," she said sternly. "Now you must be quiet so I can catch us something to eat. You play over there. Right there. And be quiet."

Teresa stood over the tumbling stream listening to the sound of water rushing to sea, the power of water rushing and tumbling. What are we running from? she asked the water. Perhaps more to the point, where was *fear* driving them?

Days passed with the dark wall of smoke always waiting, urging, pushing them forward as fast as they could go. Then one morning, they woke later than usual to a pale cloud-tossed sky, as beautiful a morning as Teresa had ever seen. Somehow they had been allowed to oversleep. Teresa stretched gratefully and the boy chattered over his breakfast of roots and onions while the horse grazed. They walked slowly to the path they had left the night before.

I don't feel . . . anything, the horse said as Teresa prepared to lift the boy to sit on his back.

She stopped. You're right, she whispered.

"What is it?" the boy also asked out loud.

Let's keep going, Teresa said to the horse. Let's see what happens.

"It's all right," she said to the boy. "Don't worry."

"What did you say to the horse?" he insisted, and she was not surprised. So he understood about that.

They traveled all day, meeting one other couple on the path, an anxious-looking man and woman who retreated into the bushes. For lunch, Teresa gathered sour berries, and she and Boy ate the roots left over from breakfast. The horse tore up handfuls of grass. Once the boy had napped, Teresa urged them onward. Let's see what happens, she said again to the horse. At a fork in the trail, they took the path that went higher, northeast.

We'll stop early, Teresa decided. We will see then.

They waited, expecting the worst. After a while, Teresa tried making another fishing net from the thready leaves of the yucca plants scattered through the scrub pine and oak. She fashioned something small and flimsy but still managed to catch two fish before the net broke. Proud of herself, she spit and roasted the trout with peppery herbs. The white meat greased her lips and flecked the boy's face.

After they had eaten, Teresa remembered something Fray Tomás had taught her, and she wove a chain of yellow daisies, putting them on the boy's head. Then she wove another one for herself. The boy frowned when she placed the leafy crown on his dark hair. But he laughed uproariously at how the yellow petals and green leaves looked on her, half-covering her ears at an angle. "You look like . . ." he giggled, but he couldn't think of anything similar in his life. No animal or person had ever worn flowers as a hat.

Teresa remembered something else, something the Moor had done when she was bored or complaining. He had called it a whirligig. She stood up to hold the boy's hands and showed him how to lean back. Leaning back, too, she twirled him in a dance until they were both dizzy. After they fell to the ground, the boy cuddled against her and she examined the bite on his arm, which was almost healed. As the air darkened, she fanned away the few mosquitoes that came to bother them.

"Am I a king now?" the boy asked, touching his crown.

"No," Teresa said, "but you are special. You have special powers. You will grow up to be an important person."

"Tell me a story," the boy said.

"I will tell you about a girl with long black hair who could swim through rivers of stone. She moved through the earth as wind moves through the branches of a tree. Once she followed a current of stone all the way to fire . . ."

11

The next day, they traveled as usual, the horse out of habit and Teresa because she wanted to find the wise woman. They were so relieved at the absence of *fear* that no one brought up the subject. Even the boy seemed unwilling to say the obvious, as if that might bring the wall of smoke back, curling behind them on the path.

Daydreaming about the wise woman, Teresa had even more questions than before. For the first time, she tried to think: where was the wise woman's village? How far north? What path should they take next? Teresa had thought she would know instinctively how to find that crumbling adobe house—that her vision in the Governor's barn would tell her where to go. Riding the horse now, she concentrated. She had to work backward through her journey with Cabeza de Vaca, Alonso del Castillo, Andrés Dorantes, and the Moor Esteban. Where had they met the Spanish slave hunters and the captain with stumps of rotting teeth? How many leagues was that from the hill where Teresa had listened to the coyote and owl? The phlox had rung like copper bells. The limestone in the earth had hissed with the sound of waves. Somewhere close, a fang-tooth mountain scratched the sky. In truth, all this had happened so long ago. She had been a child. She hadn't paid attention to distances and forks in the trail.

Where the path divided again, the horse stopped and waited for her decision.

Teresa tried to think—but a sound interrupted her, a human voice high-pitched and female.

Cautious, Teresa did not dismount. "Who's there? What's wrong?"

Get ready to run, she told the horse as she tightened her hold on the boy.

The place where they had paused was flat and grassy, a meadow fringed by a row of wind-swept pines growing close together like brush. On the other side of the meadow, the land dropped, with a view that showed a valley of irrigated green and yellow fields. Below, Teresa could see a cluster of houses, part of what she assumed to be a village. The way down to these houses looked steep but well used. The other way continued upward.

The sounds came from the brushy pine trees. Something in them moved as though an animal were struggling, and then a young woman emerged with scratched arms and twigs in her hair. Her stomach protruded, for she was very pregnant. Red designs patterned her bare breasts, and her leather skirt lifted to show strong legs and sandaled feet. Although she looked and dressed like one of the Indians in this area, she spoke Spanish.

"Please help me," she whimpered, holding her stomach. Her dark eyes shone. "Take me to the village."

Startled, Teresa lifted the boy down and slid to the ground herself. "Are you ill?" she asked. Where she came from, it was the first question everyone asked.

"No, no," the woman smiled and then made a sound again. "I am near my time. I want to be in my house."

Teresa had to wonder why the woman was not in her house now. The woman seemed to understand. "I've been gathering herbs for the birth. I misjudged and the pains have come." Her face twisted. "Please, take me home!"

Unwillingly, Teresa felt sorry for her—and curious. She had never seen a pregnant woman so close. She knew nothing about birthing. Also it seemed they must have left the *sarampión* behind. This woman, at least, didn't fear them.

"Can you ride a horse?" she asked, looking doubtfully at the huge belly.

"Oh, yes," the woman fluttered her hands. "I am fine, for the moment. I can ride, and the boy can ride with me."

Her dark eyes lingered on Boy, who leaned against Teresa's leg. Teresa turned to speak with Horse. Would he let the woman ride him?

But the gelding had backed away, his ears pointed forward.

She is not what she says, the horse said to Teresa.

"I can ride," the woman was saying out loud. "The boy and I can ride, and you can lead us. The path is steep."

Teresa felt an absence and an alarm, for the boy was no longer leaning against her. She looked down and around, and he was gone! But no, he had only moved away, too, a little distance into the meadow. He also stared suspiciously at the woman.

He knows, the horse said. He can tell. She is a shape-shifter like him.

Like him! Teresa was startled. She is a jaguar?

No, the horse hesitated. Not that. Something else.

The pregnant woman waddled closer. The horse and boy kept moving out of her reach. The boy skirted toward the brushy pine trees, while the horse went in the opposite direction back down the path. Teresa stayed where she was, blocking the woman's approach.

"What is it?" the woman wailed. Her eyes were wet, her face contorted. "Why won't you help me?"

"Who are you really?" Teresa rapped out.

The woman gave another cry and dropped to her knees. "Please," she begged. "I must get to the village. Please!"

Teresa could sense it herself now. Very slightly, the woman's shape was wrong. And there was something familiar about that wrongness. Teresa had had this bad feeling before. They all had. The curls of black smoke. The black wall of *fear*.

"Stay away!" she said, her voice shaking. What could she do? She had lost the knife. How could she defend herself or the boy? Teresa looked over at the child, who watched the scene tensely, ready to run. That was good, at least. The boy had his own means of escape. If he were frightened enough, if he were in danger, would he make the change?

On her knees, the pregnant woman lifted her hands in frustration. "Oh!" she half-snarled, half-groaned. Then she grew smoky. She thinned. She blackened. She lengthened. She rearranged herself, swirling into a new shape. Her stomach shrank. Her skin lightened, and her hair fell away. She was bald. Her eyes were blue. His eyes were blue, a pale watery color like evening light. Her leather skirt softened and expanded until it covered his body in a brown woolen cloth, the robes of a monk. The monk knelt in prayer and raised his hands, a gesture of supplication and welcome.

"Teresa," Fray Tomás said. "Help me. Take me to the village."

Teresa wanted to weep, something she had not done since her father left her. She wanted to throw her arms around the friar. He wasn't dead after all. No matter how she had behaved toward him, no matter that she refused to speak or listen, no matter her glares and hard heart, no matter how much she denied him, he had remained her friend. Always kind, always patient. He had watched over her in the Governor's house. How she missed him. How she loved him. She only realized it now.

"Walk with me to the village," Fray Tomás said. "You and the boy. We will go down the steep path together."

Teresa felt even more confused. "But why?" she stammered.

The monk shook his head affectionately, as he had done in the past. "To save their souls, of course. To bring them to

Christ. We must meet them with kindness, as they have so often met us lost in the wilderness."

The words irritated Teresa. Her father had also said that—to her and in his report to the King of Spain. What did it mean really? She didn't care about saving the souls of the villagers or anyone else. She didn't care about bringing them to Christ. Of course, Fray Tomás cared about that because he was a monk. Fray Tomás had loved the bleeding heart of Christ and the whitewashed adobe chapel and the comfort of Mass and the boys and girls he had taught to read. Fray Tomás had surely gone to Heaven after he died, and Teresa didn't begrudge him that. The monk was with his beloved Christ now.

The monk was dead. Teresa remembered his body in the chapel, the black blood leaking from his nose and mouth. In her vision, she had seen his soul slip away, a yellow sheen. This was not Fray Tomás.

Get on my back, the horse urged. I'll take you away!

Teresa looked for the boy, who had moved even closer to the line of pine trees, far from the monk but also far from the horse.

"Let us get the boy." Fray Tomás rose from his knees and adjusted his woolen robe. "We will walk together."

"No," Teresa shouted as the man took a step toward the child. "Get away from him!"

The horse lifted his front legs and drummed his hooves on the ground.

"Teresa, what is wrong with you?" the friar asked with a deep disappointment in his voice. He lifted a pale hand to brush his bald head and then let the hand drop. He stared at her sorrowfully. "What have I done to offend you?"

"What are you really?" Teresa asked, not expecting an answer. She glanced at the boy and spoke to him urgently, hoping he was old enough to understand. "If you have to run, run. Do what you have to do."

"Oh!" The monk theatrically shook his fists. "I must get to the village." He shifted again. He grew smoky, disappearing and reappearing. He became tall and short and tall and short and tall and short and stopped when he was average height, and completely naked. His wide shoulders and chest were those of a man who had once been strong and well muscled, but now his collar bones stuck out like two jutting stones. His ribs looked like the parts of a musical instrument. His stomach curved inward like a hollow bowl. His arms and legs were spiky branches, his gray face hollowed, his hair a wispy cloud. Teresa could see the sores that covered his scalp. They covered his face, too, and ran down the length of his body—rashes, welts, leaking pustules. There was no way to know his race, Spanish or Indian, Mayan or Opata. His eyes glittered. His hands shook.

He was Plague.

His voice sounded harsh from the lesions in his throat and the weakening of his windpipe. "You know who I am," he said and grinned, his mouth bloody. "Take me to the village!" he commanded.

Teresa found her own voice, "Go!"

The boy turned into the line of pine trees and disappeared.

12

Teresa saw the boy blur as he moved. She thought she saw the flick of a tail and heard the rustle of fur through low-hanging branches. She knew the jaguar would soon be flying through the pine and scrub-brush forest, twisting around trees, humping up slopes, skidding down inclines. She strained to see into the shadows. He was gone. He was safe.

She turned back to where Plague stood before her. He was gone, too.

What happened? she asked the horse.

He disappeared, the horse answered.

The boy, you mean?

No, the shape-shifter. The old man.

"Plague," Teresa said out loud.

She was not afraid of Plague. Her hard heart protected her. Plague could not harm her, but he could harm many others. The housekeeper seemed to be next to Teresa now, whispering in her ear. The housekeeper was no fool. Her family had kept themselves alive by serving the cruel Aztecs and then the cruel Spanish. They bowed to their masters, but they kept their eyes and ears open, watching and listening. The housekeeper had been smart and practical. She sized up the situation, explaining it to Teresa: Horse and Boy and Teresa had left the villages of *sarampión* behind, with Plague harrying and driving them as fast as they could go. This far north, people were not yet suffering from the most recent epidemic, not yet dying, not yet grieving. Of course, Plague had wanted to walk with Teresa and Boy into this new village below. Because Plague needed a human being at his side. He needed someone to bring the disease, the way the Spanish had brought it when they came to the New World.

Teresa saw again the hares running from bush to bush into the hunter's hand. And she saw, too, that if they did what Plague wanted, he would leave them alone. She and Horse could go into the village with Plague, and then Plague would stay behind with the suffering and dying people. He would have what he wanted. She would be free of him. She remembered the song: *Sarampión toca la puerta. Viruela dice:¿Quién es? Y Escarlatina contesta: Aquí estamos los tres.* Measles knocks at the door. Smallpox asks, Who's there? And Scarlet Fever replies, All three of us are here!

She shook her head. She had walked with a healer. Men and women jumped up, saying they felt completely well. Even the man with an arrowhead in his chest had risen from his grass mat saying he felt strong and well, while his wife and children looked relieved. They celebrated with yellow tea, dancing under the river of stars, singing and laughing. Her father had looked on, smiling at his daughter. Whatever else he had been, her father had been a healer.

She had to find the boy. Teresa felt a small sense of victory. The boy was safe. And Plague was gone for the moment. His trick had failed.

Teresa examined the ground where the boy had been and soon saw what she was looking for. Paw prints. The front heel pads as wide as her hand, the toes in a curve, the claws retracted. Crouching, she began to follow the prints into the trees.

What are you doing? Horse called from behind. Where are you going?

The horse sounded anxious, and Teresa came back out. I have to get the boy, she explained.

That is crazy, the horse said. That is supremely ridiculous and beyond the realm of common sense. That animal is many miles away.

Then I'll have to walk many miles, Teresa replied.

He'll turn around and eat you! The horse snorted to show his full displeasure and swished his tail back and forth.

No, he won't, Teresa said. Of course, he won't.

But she wasn't completely sure about that.

Plop, plop. The horse defecated, filling the air with an acrid but not unpleasant odor. Perhaps he had no choice in the matter, or perhaps he wanted to make a point. Teresa came forward into the meadow and stroked Horse's muzzle. She did this automatically as she whispered, you can't come with me. It's too brushy. You have to wait here.

I don't want to wait. The horse whinnied, perhaps thinking of his first master.

Yes, yes, but look at this nice grass, this tall sweet grass. Find a place to rest, away from the path. Don't let people see you. Go find water, and then return here. Wait for me here.

He might come back.

Plague can't hurt you, Teresa said. I am counting on you, she crooned as she stroked the fine fur and scratched the skin between the horse's ears. I may be gone a long time. When I come back with the boy, we will talk about what to do next.

He will eat you for supper, the horse predicted, and you will cry out for me in heartrending tones.

At first the tracks were not hard to follow in the soft dirt under the pine and oak, places where the jaguar had pushed with his back feet in a hurry to get away, where his toes dug into the earth and disturbed the debris of needles and leaves. Soon, though, Teresa had to bend and squirm through the low branches, weaving through the resinous trees and skirting the occasional prickly pear or sharp-tipped yucca—just as the jaguar had skirted them as he ran from the frightening scene in the meadow. As she followed the prints, she breathed in the sharp smell of pine sap and the decaying litter of the forest floor. She had to watch carefully the ever-changing but ever-the-same patterns on the ground: dirt, stone, leaf, needle, and there, a slight indentation, the curve of a heel pad. She heard a jay's squawk and the rustle of mice.

Slowly, the circle of her thoughts wound down. So many questions and decisions to make. Why had Plague chosen them? How could she find the wise woman and her village? How could she enter the wise woman's village without bringing along Plague? Slowly, those concerns drifted away. She only had to follow these tracks, these marks in the ground. She only had to move through the trees like an animal herself, hunting another animal.

After half a league, the prints left the shelter of stunted pine, and the jaguar was running down a rocky slope across boulders of granite encrusted with yellow lichen. Sometimes Teresa could not find a mark for long stretches, and she had to rely on her intuition, her sense of where the big cat would go. Sometimes she had to backtrack, and for a while she was afraid she had lost him completely and was completely lost herself. Scanning the ground and then the horizon, she stood on an overlook from where she could see an expanse of canyons and jumbled hills covered with juniper and thorn bush. The village and its green and yellow fields were already behind her. Where was the boy in this rolling stretch of land? Teresa felt like cursing, as she had often heard women in the kitchen curse when they cut a finger or ruined a dish.

She closed her eyes and concentrated on an image of the boy's face: the rounded cheeks, the long dark eyelashes, the grin that sometimes made her grin because—because he looked so pleased with himself, so ridiculously smug. She concentrated on his giggle and the way he had preened in his crown of yellow daisies. She called out to him. Then she plodded back up the slope, turned to her right, and found another track, a fresh print that led to another and another.

The jaguar was moving into the canyon below. Scrambling up a boulder, Teresa stretched her back and squinted and peered. Against a distant rock cliff, the edge of something showed green, the top of a cottonwood with the bright leaves of summer. A cottonwood tree meant water, likely a spring. The jaguar was going there to drink.

Teresa gathered her energy for the descent, down the steep crumbly slope. Her stomach rumbled. They had not yet stopped for lunch when Plague had tried to trick them in the meadow. Now it was many hours later, late afternoon, and her body wanted food. She envied the horse, grazing on tall sweet grass as he waited. She felt a little sorry for herself: tired and hungry and thirsty. Stumbling on rocks, slipping on gravel, she fell twice, starting small avalanches in the loose stone and scraping her hands. For some sections, she went down on her buttocks, half-sliding and hoping not to slide into the needles of a cholla cactus. More than ever, she was grateful for her sturdy yucca sandals, given to her as part of a servant's "pay" for working in the Governor's kitchen. The rest of her pay was a leather skirt, a cotton shirt, all the food she could eat, and a place to sleep. It hadn't been such a bad bargain, she realized. Certainly she had grown used to eating a meal every few hours, whenever she wanted, and as much as she wanted. At this moment, she would give almost anything for a tortilla and bowl of stew. Or slices of cantaloupe. A piece of bread baked fresh for the Governor every morning. Porridge. Eggs. A turkey wing.

Teresa blew on her stinging bleeding hands and half-fell to the bottom of the long slope. For a while, she stood with rubbery legs in the sandy arroyo. Without much hope, she looked around for berries or roots or a small animal to kill. There was nothing to eat, nothing at all. But there were more tracks farther down the canyon, very clear in the white sand. The jaguar had come this way, too. The boy was nearby.

Keeeeen. Screeeeee. A pair of falcons screamed at her angrily. The low sandstone cliffs of the box canyon were pockmarked with the caves and white-smeared holes where these birds nested. Off and on as she walked, she saw the prints of the big cat. But she didn't really need to look for them now. She knew where he was going.

The canyon walls narrowed, the shadows deepened, and the sun had dropped close to setting by the time she reached the spring. The world ended here in a half-circle of red rock, the colors burnished and striated, orange and brown and cinnamon. Above these towers, the azure sky darkened with the coming twilight. Below, the water of the pond reflected perfectly the shape of the cottonwood tree, the leaves of the tree rustling and swaying in a breeze, the green leaves a promise of everything good. Grass grew around the edges of the pond, along with wildflowers, yellow and white and red, dotting the ground like stars in the sky.

As soon as she saw that blue water and great overarching tree, Teresa's weariness fell away like a tossed blanket. Her feet weren't so bruised and sore. Her scraped hands hurt less. Even her hard heart seemed to lift and soar. She stared, puzzled at her reaction, and then she knew—this is how she had always imagined Heaven. Whenever Fray Tomás spoke of Paradise, whenever he praised Eden and its joys, this is what she saw.

The air felt freshly cool on her face as she went to drink from the shallow pool, then to stand on the bank and look searchingly about, scanning the nearby rock, alert for that pattern of the jaguar's spots, the black and gold fur. Likely he was resting in one of these darkened alcoves, resting and waiting for her. Perhaps he was scared, remembering Plague. It's time to wake up, she thought. Time to come back. She called out, "Boy! Boy!"

A panting noise answered. *Hunh, hunh, hunh.*

Teresa startled and turned. Across the green grass, from a shadowed cave in the red rock, the jaguar appeared, coughed, and stared. Bending his body and head lower to the ground, he inched toward her, his muscled legs tensed. His mottled coat glowed in the dimming light. His long tail flickered back and forth without a sound, and his big round eyes watched her intently, focused on her alone. She was all that mattered to him.

Sit still, he said. Don't move. Don't be afraid.

And Teresa was still, fascinated by those amber eyes, so intent, so focused.

This is your destiny, the jaguar said.

No, Teresa thought. Blinked and shook herself. It was not her destiny at all. Stop it, she said to the jaguar. Stop that. The animal paused, but only slightly. One paw lifted and moved back down and the next paw lifted, all so silently, bringing him forward, closer to her.

I remember you, the jaguar said. You are the human who spoke to me before, when I changed back.

Change back now, Teresa ordered. I want to see the boy.

The jaguar crouched lower and opened his mouth in a snarl, so that Teresa could see his pointed teeth. His blocky head and wide nose made him look imperious, like a king. I am no longer the boy, he snarled. I am myself, me. I am hungry, and I will eat you.

No! Teresa said. She made herself speak calmly, firmly. I am the boy's friend. I take care of him.

I am no longer the boy, the jaguar repeated. He huffed in a series of angry *hunh! hunh! hunh!* The boy no longer needs you. The boy is better off with me. We will never change back again. We will eat you and drink you and sleep in the cave.

109

Teresa stiffened. She called again—not to the jaguar, but to the child. Remember the fish we caught together? Remember how good it tasted? Remember how we laughed and laughed? Change back now and we will fish here in this pond and then we will build a fire and sleep and go back to the horse. Remember how the horse let you ride him?

The jaguar wrinkled his flat nose. I like fish, he said. But there are no fish in this pond. I don't smell any fish, only frogs and insects.

Then we will catch a rabbit, Teresa said. We will roast it for supper. I'll tell you a story about a fiesta. A beautiful fiesta with lots of food.

A fiesta? the jaguar faltered.

A party with music and jugglers and chocolate and tortillas. You remember eating tortillas? You remember dancing! You remember being human.

I don't! The jaguar sat back on his haunches and moved his head back and forth. He opened his mouth to gather in more scent from the air. He didn't know what to do. *Hunh. Hunh.* He huffed.

You remember your mother, Teresa said firmly. You remember your Mamá. What happened to her? Where is she?

Teresa found herself entering the jaguar's mind more forcefully than she had ever entered the mind of the horse or any other animal. She wanted to know more about the boy, how he shape-shifted and why. She wanted to know what had happened to his mother and father. Her curiosity and fear formed an edge that she used to move deep into the animal's thoughts.

There she felt a whirling and a turning. She was staring out of yellow eyes. She saw the flutter of the cottonwood tree. She saw the shifting shadows along the rock walls. She saw a human girl standing by the pond, a human girl colored in shades of gray, each shade distinct. Even in the dimming sunset, she could see perfectly—the sharp detail of the girl's stained

110

clothes, her hair coming loose and unbraided, the four tattoos on each cheek.

The vertical pupil of her eye widened to take in more light.

Teresa knew now what the jaguar knew. He was not like other animals, for he flickered in and out of existence whenever the boy changed, and even in this, he was new and different—he was a mistake. A Mayan shaman did not enter the Jaguar God until adolescence. But the boy had changed early because the power was strong in him and because his parents did not have their village to guide them and because the rituals had not been done correctly. If they had not been taken north by the Spanish, they would have known what herbs to use and what ceremonies to perform. The boy would have grown old enough to control the jaguar, and the Jaguar God would have taught him how to change and when. Now it was too late.

What do you mean? Teresa asked the animal even as she looked through his yellow eyes.

I am here now. I won't go back.

And you want what? Teresa pressed.

I want life! I want to be!

But while you live, what happens to the boy? Where is he?

The jaguar gave a mental shrug. He sleeps. He sleeps inside me safe and well.

Teresa thought about that. She looked out at the jaguar's world, the prey on the bank of the pond—a human girl easily caught and killed, a delicious girl filled with blood, her flesh nourishing. She saw the fluttering cottonwood leaves, and she had the urge to bat them with her paw although she knew this was silly, for they were too high up. She scanned the rock cliffs. A falcon watched anxiously from its nest. She lifted her nose and opened her mouth and breathed in.

Her senses exploded. Now she could smell what the jaguar could smell, intoxicating odors deeper and richer than anything she had experienced before, layers of smell she could read like

Fray Tomás had read the words in her father's book: the wet decay of leaves; the urine of a coyote; the death fear of a mouse; the sweet cloy of the datura flower opening to attract the night moth; the poison in the flower's petals and leaves; water and mud and insects and toads; lizards that should be eaten only if necessary; the wind carrying the smell of other animals; the wind itself; and the girl, of course, always the girl with her juicy flesh. The girl smelled incredibly good.

Teresa felt the world, immediate and joyous, pressing on her senses. There was no doubt what she should do. She should crouch and spring and eat the girl. That would give her more life, more of this world!

I understand, she said to the jaguar. You would have the boy sleep forever so you can live in his place. You are not willing to share this life with him.

He is not willing to share with me, the jaguar protested. The shamans would have me come out once a month, roaming the forest for a single night. They would have me under the boy's control, under their control, ready to do their bidding to protect the village. They would have me retreat meekly like a rabbit or mouse whenever they command.

That's how it should be, Teresa said.

But that is not how it is, the jaguar replied. I have come early, and I am stronger than the boy. I am stronger than you. *I will have my life.*

Wait! Teresa said. She reached out for the boy. She tried to wake him, to concentrate on his face, to make him hear her. You remember your father, she insisted. You remember your mother. You lived with them among the Spanish *hidalgos* and slave hunters. You remember them.

The jaguar shook his head and the long length of his body as if trying to shake off a spray of water.

But he did remember. His father and mother had been slaves, although not in the silver mines, branded, overworked,

112

and soon dead. They had been the personal slaves of a Spanish *alcalde mayor*, the main official in a small town, a man who treated them well and who let their little boy run freely in the house and barracks making friends with everyone from household cook to captain himself. The boy had been happy, tossed into the air by his father, cuddled and fed by his mother. Even the slave hunters had petted him, letting him play with their whips and swords, the swords so heavy he could barely lift them.

One day, his father had seen that his son had the shaman's power. His father was not surprised, for his father's uncle had had the power, too. So his father had taken him behind the barn and made him drink a bitter liquid and had cut his hand so that blood dripped freely into a cup. His mother watched and cried because she was afraid. His mother's mother also had entered the Jaguar God once a month, roaming the forest near their village and keeping the village safe from other animals— but that was in a place where people understood such things. His mother had cried, "They will think it is witchcraft!" and his father had held his son close. "We will protect him," he said.

Yes, Teresa urged, that is your real life.

The jaguar growled, remembering. But they didn't protect him, the jaguar hissed through yellow teeth. The rituals didn't work. They were not done correctly in a circle of shamans. I came too soon, and I am too strong. His mother and father died. Even the slave hunters died. There is nothing left for him in the human world.

The jaguar remembered, and Teresa remembered. The Indians in that area had risen up as they sometimes did, tired of the iron fists of the conquistadors, with their new rules and new religion. Perhaps these Opatas had found some special power. Perhaps they were led by a man or woman who claimed a magic they believed could overthrow the magic of the Spanish, the pitiless magic of *sarampión* and *viruela*, and so they had stormed the town of the *alcalde mayor*. Without doubt, that man had been terribly shocked, for he thought himself a benevolent ruler. His men of arms were also shocked, cut down as they slept, stabbed in the heart with a stone knife or smashed on the head with a heavy rock. The Mayan slaves had also been killed. They meant nothing to the Indians here. They were foreigners just as much as the Spanish.

The boy had seen everything. He had woken in the night needing to urinate, and he had gone out alone without waking his mother, exploring alone as he sometimes did around the barracks and barn, letting his eyes adjust to the darkness. He saw the shadows of shadows creeping into the compound. He heard cries and curses as the Spanish woke and fought and died. He saw the *alcalde mayor* dragged out from his house into the dirt yard, near the fruit trees. The Opatas slit his throat and let the blood water the trees. They dragged out the *alcalde mayor*'s family, his wife and teenage daughters, and all the servants and slaves, and they slit their throats, too, and let their blood water the trees.

When the boy heard his mother screaming, just before she died, he ran from his hiding place near some barrels of grain. The blood-spattered men saw him. "Another one!" they shouted to each other and threw his dead mother on the ground next to his dead father. With jokes and terrifying smiles, they came for him.

But they were not smiling when he changed. They drew back then, and some of them ran away. The jaguar wanted to chase those men. He almost rushed forward, almost lashed out biting and clawing. But he was bewildered and full of a wild mourning, and he ran away instead, fleeing the bodies on the ground. He lived as a jaguar for many days, until Teresa found him and spoke to him.

You brought the boy back, the jaguar accused her.

114

And I will bring him back again, Teresa insisted. She understood that if she waited any longer, she would be seduced by the smells of the jaguar's world, by his hunger and anticipation of the girl's flesh—flesh that was her own, she reminded herself. She had to leave the jaguar's mind, and she had to take the boy with her. Wake up, she said, and reached out.

Teresa knew now what the jaguar knew, everything that had happened before the boy's change, and so she knew the boy's name, what his mother and father had called him, all their love in that single word. "Pomo!" she cried. "Pomo, wake up!"

13

The boy complained as Teresa bathed his face with water from the pond. He pushed his head against her stomach, and she held him tightly. She didn't know how much he remembered from being a jaguar and running from Plague, or how much he remembered of that night when his mother and father were killed. She didn't know how to talk to him about his parents, and so she didn't. She only held him and made a soothing noise.

After a while, he sneezed and drew away. "I'm hungry," he said.

Darkness had settled into the canyon, and briefly Teresa wished for the jaguar's eyes so she could see well enough to hunt and gather. That was impossible now, and they would have to go without food. "I know," she told the boy. "The morning will be better."

In the morning, she found a packrat's nest, with a packrat inside that they roasted for breakfast. The rat also had a cache of pine nuts, and they added these to the stringy meat. Afterward Teresa reknotted the tinderbox in her cotton shirt.

"We'll eat again soon," she promised as they walked up the canyon. The large trumpet-shaped datura flowers, white and lavender, were still open, exuding their rich scent. She pointed these out to the boy and warned him they were poisonous, every flower, leaf, and root, causing hallucinations and death. He nodded without interest.

"Did you already know that?" Teresa asked.

The boy shrugged—no. It seemed he knew little from his time as a jaguar. He is truly asleep, Teresa thought, and wondered if there were rituals that would help him. Perhaps the shamans of his people would know how to keep the boy awake when he entered the Jaguar God. Perhaps the wise woman at the Opata village would know what to do to help the boy control the animal. The boy's jaguar—Pomo's jaguar, Teresa corrected herself—had come too early and was too strong for a child. She couldn't let him change back again.

"You must not change back," she scolded as they reached the trail she had made coming down into the canyon. The boy looked at her, surprised by her tone. "Pomo," she said more gently, "the animal in you is too strong for you. You must not take that shape." The boy shrugged, confused, then stubborn. He would not talk about it.

They climbed slowly, for his legs were short, and he was also careless, starting rock slides that threatened Teresa until she learned to climb beside and not below him. "I'm hungry," the boy said again at the top.

An hour later, they saw a circle of vultures dipping and soaring in the blue sky. The carrion that attracted the scavengers was in the direction they traveled, and they detoured through a patch of thorn bushes. Closer to the carcass, Teresa could smell that the deer was badly rotted. Still, she wondered if she could find some good meat somewhere before remembering she had no knife or even the flinted rock she had made earlier. She had no way to separate good meat from bad. Pomo suggested grabbing a leg and wrenching it from its socket. But then they would have to stop and build a fire, Teresa explained, and the rotten flesh might make them sick. She was in a hurry to get back to the meadow. For a moment, she paused, watching the vultures stab and tear, jealous of their sharp beaks.

"No," she said regretfully. "We'll find something else later on."

Next they were lucky when their detour brought them by a field of prickly pear, its oblong fruit ripe and red, not yet discovered by a family of peccary or the long-nosed coati. This was a very satisfying lunch, with Teresa scraping away the fine prickles and giving first one fruit to Pomo then one for herself. They alternated like this through half the plants, spitting out the tiny black seeds and savoring the pulp until their stomachs were overfull. Before moving on, Teresa took off her cotton shirt and tied it into a gathering bag she could carry. The rest of the fruit would make a good supper.

They walked all day, past the vista of jumbled hills and into the forest of pine trees and scrub brush. Toward the end Teresa had to force the boy, pushing and prodding with her sore hands and sarcastic tongue while he whined and complained. His legs were tired. His stomach hurt. He wanted to rest. He wanted to stop.

"Stop and I'll leave you," Teresa threatened. Pomo began to cry, and so she came back and carried him the last bit, crouching under the low pine branches, seeing the jaguar's tracks as well as her own from the day before. The boy felt like a sack of rocks. The gathering bag of fruit hung awkwardly across her chest. She felt as though every root and stone were trying to trip her. They neared the meadow by the path just as the sun was setting again, and Teresa found herself praying to Fray Tomás and Jesus and the wise woman all together. What if Horse had decided not to wait? What would they do if the animal wasn't there?

The western sky blazed with color, the remnant of a thunderstorm lit by the sun's last rays, billowing white clouds edged in pink. Shafts of light pointed to the earth like fingers of an outstretched hand as Teresa staggered from the forest into the meadow, too tired to look for Plague or other dangers. She let the boy slide to the ground and called for Horse, and then out loud, "Horse, Horse!"

As always, the boy said he was hungry. Teresa told him to sit at the edge of shadow where the forest and meadow met. Again she used a stone to rub off the thorns of the prickly pear fruit, which was good for their thirst as well as their hunger. She knew she had to be patient. The horse might be away drinking or exploring. He might be gone for hours or even days. Or he might come ambling up the path any minute, for it was almost dark.

So! Horse grumped, as she petted his face and neck.

I found the boy, Teresa stated the obvious. And you look well rested and fed. She paused. Has there been any sign of *him*?

No, the horse still sounded annoyed. But there have been others intruding into my peace of mind. A hunting party. A trading party. A pack of noisy chattering women looking for something. I spent half my time hiding in bushes like a drunken foolscap.

We need a knife, Teresa spoke absently, thinking of the trading party.

There will be knives in the village. But you have nothing to offer for them, the horse reminded her.

Teresa shook her head and looked around for Pomo, who was sitting where she had left him, half-asleep, his face smeared with red juice. She was certain that if they went into the village, they would find Plague suddenly walking beside them. If they approached a trading party, they would find Plague again among them. She couldn't be near people now. But—Teresa almost growled—she wasn't willing to wander the rest of her life without speaking or seeing another human being.

Plague will come back, Horse interrupted her thoughts, blowing thoughtful bubbles from his nostrils. He will come back for the boy. One victim is better than nothing.

Appalled, Teresa stared at the gelding and then turned in all directions, scanning the meadow and forest and path. Of course, Horse was right. She should have seen this herself. If she had left the boy sleeping in the Jaguar God, at least he would be protected from disease. She had brought Pomo back only so Plague could take him!

She had to find the wise woman first. Not just for her own questions, but for Pomo, too. She had to find someone who could help them.

Let's go now, she exclaimed. Let's get out of here.

The day is over, Horse neighed.

There is a moon tonight, Teresa said, a full moon. Let's go when it rises. Let's see if you can outrun Plague.

To outrun Plague! Teresa challenged the horse. He had fought in many important battles. He had crossed the ocean. He was a *hidalgo*'s mount, a member of his captain's army. This would be a great opportunity, a test, a deed, something he could boast about the rest of his life. To outrun Plague. This would ensure him a place of glory!

Enough, Horse said, pawing the ground. You don't need to convince me. I'll carry you and the boy. I've ridden in moonlight before.

As fast as you can, Teresa whispered into the horse's ear, as she clamped her knees tightly across his back and pressed down on Pomo so he wouldn't fall. Plague could return at any moment. She felt the animal grin in her mind just before he began to gallop. He had rested and eaten for almost two days. He was ready to run.

The moon followed them the whole way, fat and orange, a cheerful companion. The path also seemed to spur them forward as it angled down from the mountains onto a broad level plain. Eventually, of course, although not soon, the horse tired and had to walk, almost until dawn. Then when the gelding scented water—a stream neither wide nor deep—he insisted on stopping. There is less water ahead, he warned. All night, I have smelled the desert.

Teresa lifted Pomo and let him drop to the ground. When she got off the horse herself, every part of her body ached. She had also seen how the moonlight shone now on cactus and rock, with fewer pine and scrub oak. They had been descending steadily, the path forking more than once. She had always picked the northern route, north and east, and this route led them away from the pine-topped mountains with their cool breezes and clear waters running to the sea.

"We'll drink here," she said to Pomo, who had slept for much of the ride. Later in the morning, she would look for buffalo gourds. If she could kill a large enough animal, she could use its stomach or bladder to carry water, too. If only she had a real knife, she thought, something better and sharper than her cutting tool.

As she found a place for them to rest, a grassy spot of earth under a hackberry tree, Teresa worried about that lost knife, about what they would eat next, about buffalo gourds. Even if she could carry water for herself and Pomo, she could not carry enough for Horse. He would have to find a spring or creek in the desert, for himself and for them as well. She wondered how big this desert was and how many days it would take to cross it. She wondered if one of them should stand guard in case there were wolves or lions or slavers nearby. She wondered if they could really outrun Plague. Was any place safe from *him*?

But north—through the desert—was the way that led to the wise woman. That was the way they had to go. She wondered . . . head on the ground now, eyes closed . . . and then she was asleep, Pomo curled against her thigh, the horse standing and sleeping close by.

Long past sunrise, when she woke, Plague was there, too. He sat on a rock, watching them, his arms wrapped around his knees. He waited for her in the form of her mother.

At first, Teresa just stared at the woman. There was something so familiar about those dark brown eyes and lips curving up. Teresa blinked and half-rose on her elbows. The woman was naked except for a grass skirt. She smelled of salt and fish, and her head had been flattened slightly in the back. She was still almost young, older than Teresa but not yet middle-aged. Her brown face crinkled into laugh lines when she smiled.

"Te-re-sa!" her mother said in a lilting voice.

"Mother," Teresa whispered. "Where . . . where is the baby?"

"The baby . . ." the woman stopped.

"My sister?" Teresa prompted and stood, careful not to disturb Pomo. The horse nickered low, also awake.

"Let's talk about you," Teresa's mother said gently. "It has been so long. You left without saying good-bye."

A shudder went through Teresa's hard heart.

But "You are so young," Teresa said. "You can't be my mother. Where is my sister? My mother would know this."

"Te-re-sa," her mother lilted, "aren't you happy to see me?"

Teresa took a breath to steady herself. "My sister is dead, isn't she? And you, my mother. My mother is also dead. I think you can only take the shape of people you have killed."

"No," her mother sighed, "you are wrong about that."

Plague shook his head sadly before continuing. "But, yes, your mother is dead and your baby sister. After you left without saying good-bye, another poor shipwrecked stranger came to their tribe, and they welcomed him, too. He also brought the sickness that made their skin burn and their bodies shake as though the Bad Spirit were rattling them from the inside. Many of them died. All your family. Your grandfather. Your aunts. The stranger killed them."

"You killed them," Teresa replied, not knowing how to feel. She hadn't thought about her family in so long. "Plague killed them."

"Perhaps," her mother conceded. She gestured, still gentle, still sad. "But the Spanish have done other bad things, haven't they? They took your friends as slaves, all the poor people who traveled with your father. The captain took them. And they sneered at you. Alonso del Castillo and Andrés Dorantes. They mocked you. They stole your father away with their talk of gold, their sweet-smelling wardrobes and chairs and *escritorios.*"

Teresa tried to think about buffalo gourds. Could she find a gourd in which to carry water? The sun shone brightly on the grass and yellow flowers by the stream.

"Listen to me," her mother coaxed. "Only a few leagues away to the west, a group of Spanish slave hunters are herding their slaves to Mexico City. You can join them now, you and the boy. That will be your revenge, to see them sicken, too. You can watch their skin burn, watch them shake! That will revenge your mother. That will revenge your baby sister. Take me to these men."

Pomo was waking up, murmuring and stretching. When he saw the woman on the rock, he froze like a spotted fawn.

"It's all right," Teresa said quickly. "I won't let him near you." She took the boy's hand and pulled him to his feet. Step by step, they backed up, toward the horse. "The Spanish are protected," she told her mother, just as a distraction. "They don't die of the *sarampión* or *viruela.* They don't worry about *escarlatina.*"

"Some of them do," Plague said with a shrug. "Some of them can still get sick. And their slaves will certainly get very sick. Their slaves will burn and shake and that will make their owners very unhappy. In the meantime, we will go together into the next town, and then all the way to Mexico City. That is a place I love very much."

"I won't help you," Teresa said. Get ready, she told the horse.

Her mother sighed and watched, and Teresa understood that Plague had limits. She or the boy had to go to him. Maybe they had to touch or be touched by him. Also, although Plague was clever and sly, he had forgotten about her baby sister. And his plan to sicken the Spanish slave hunters was not very persuasive. He hadn't remembered that they would make her and Pomo slaves, too, and that the boy would also get sick. Why would she risk that for revenge? Plague did not know humans as well as he thought.

When Teresa could feel Horse's breath on her neck, she turned and lifted Pomo to his back. Grabbing the horse's mane, she scrambled up behind, and Horse wheeled, and then they were thundering on their way north and east across the desert plain. The path was gone now. They would have to use the sun and stars for direction.

14

All that day, she urged the horse forward even though he was tired from yesterday's travel, even though Pomo was cranky and restless, even though her head ached and her eyes felt as if they had been rubbed with sand. Let's go, Teresa said when the horse slowed. The desert is what *he* is avoiding. He can't cross the desert after us.

That is not true, the horse replied. You know that is not true.

Teresa frowned because Horse was right. Why would Plague hate the desert—except that the desert had so few people. And Plague needed people. Plague loved people.

The wise woman will help us, she said confidently to the gelding. We have to find her before Plague finds us again and thinks of some new trick. We have to cross this desert before we die of thirst. Hurry! she commanded over the pain of her headache.

Horse neighed angrily. I know how fast I can go in this heat!

"I want to get off," Pomo said, drumming his feet against the horse's ribs. "I don't want to ride anymore."

"Hush," Teresa said, "Horse is scenting for water."

They were all so thirsty. The desert blazed so much hotter than the mountains, and they had left the stream before they had

had a chance to drink. Teresa could feel the bare skin burning on her arms and face and sandaled feet, and she knew the same thing was happening to Pomo, who was completely naked. She should make Horse stop so that she could give Pomo her cotton shirt stained with prickly pear juice. She should find Pomo some clothes of his own, and she wondered what happened to the cotton shirts and yucca sandals of the Mayan shamans when they shape-shifted. Did they tear and break and tangle in the jaguar's limbs? Did the shape-shifting jaguar run through the forest wearing the rags of a leather skirt? Stupid, Teresa scolded herself. The shamans undressed first. They had rituals. They knew what to do. Oh, it was so hot!

They rode past cholla and ocotillo and the short humped cactus. Teresa craned her neck looking for prickly pear. That would save them. The fruits of the tall-limbed cactus were also beginning to ripen, and she searched for those plants as well.

In the late afternoon, the horse found a spring. The seep of water was surrounded by clumps of yellow grass and animal tracks hardened in drying mud. After drinking her fill, Teresa went to search for food and found a few red currant berries. On a nearby hill, a jojoba bush had ripened nuts, crunchy and oily. She and Pomo ate those and drank again from the tiny seep and then Teresa was eager to move on—to cross the desert and find the wise woman.

But the horse refused to travel further that day. He needed rest.

In the morning, he went reluctantly and only because he had grazed all the dry yellow grass. There was nothing left for him to eat.

"I don't want to ride," Pomo said as Teresa lifted the boy onto the horse's back. Teresa's cotton shirt covered him now from neck to feet, and Teresa was in a bad mood with only her leather skirt and dabs of mud protecting her bare breasts. Her efforts to find a buffalo gourd had failed, and they still had no way to carry water. Despite all the tracks near the seep, she hadn't seen a rabbit or packrat or anything to stone for their supper or breakfast. All the currant berries and jojoba nuts were gone. Like Horse, they had nothing to eat.

"We'll find something later," she muttered to herself.

"I want to get off," Pomo began though they had not yet started.

The day seemed even more miserably hot than the day before, and with each hour, they were thirstier and hungrier, their rumps and thighs chafed and bruised bumping against Horse's bony back. A heat rash broke out on the boy's face, and he complained continuously. The sun beat down like something that hated them. The air felt thick and solid. Mirages shimmered in the shape of towering buildings or mountains or blue ponds just ahead. But none of these things were real. The ponds, especially, were not real.

By sunset, Horse had not yet smelled water. He shambled along, step, step, step, stumble, stumble, stumble. Teresa could feel his exhaustion. We should stop, she said at last.

No, the horse whispered, surprising her. We will use the moonlight. We should keep going. Teresa swayed on the gelding's back, holding on to Pomo. Here and there, she spotted the humped barrel cactus. She knew that a thirsty traveler could break open this plant and use its pulp for liquid. But if they drank the mashed pulp on an empty stomach, they would get even sicker, defecating dirty water. They needed food first.

She swayed and dreamed of a pool below a cottonwood tree.

Once again, moonlight silvered the desert plants and rocks. It was beautiful and familiar, as if she had seen all this before, the silver moon, these silver plants. Of course, she had—she remembered now—not on a horse, not with a boy, but with her father and Andrés Dorantes and Alonso del Castillo and the Moor Esteban. They had often walked by moonlight, her father humming a Spanish song. *Río de Sevilla, de barco lleno, ha pasado el alma, no pasa el cuerpo . . .*

Horse plodded through the night, and when the sun rose, he said he had to find shade. He could no longer travel in the daylight. The horse stumbled to the overhang of a boulder that half-sheltered a scraggly mesquite tree. Once Teresa and the boy dismounted, she realized that they would not be riding again. The animal was at the end of his strength. He could barely speak to her, his thoughts blurred. They would have to walk now.

Teresa wondered, with shame, if she should have offered to do this earlier. She wondered how easily, how quickly, the horse would be traveling through the desert if he were not carrying them.

Pomo whispered something in a cracked voice as they settled under the tree branches, leaving the shade of the boulder for the horse. The boy was pleading for water, water and food. Teresa looked about, but all the mesquite beans had fallen to the ground and been eaten by animals. The horse stood nearby, too tired to try the tough yellow grass that grew up sparsely.

"It's all right," Teresa lied to the boy. "Go to sleep."

Pomo coughed and she saw it—a glimmer of yellow in the boy's dark eyes, a shading into liquid green-gold. The child was thirsty and hungry enough to change. Now Teresa could hear the animal's voice. I have you, and I have the horse, the jaguar counted up his treasure. Plenty of flesh, plenty of blood.

No! Teresa shouted. Horse jerked awake.

No, Teresa said, and with all her strength she pushed the jaguar down deep into the boy. She denied him. She stopped his breath. She strangled him half to death, or maybe all the way to death, for he disappeared—growling. He could not have the boy. He could not have her. He could not have the horse.

"We will find another way," she told Pomo.

The dark eyes lost their shine and only Pomo looked back at her, wet-lashed, woe-be-gone, trusting. "Go to sleep," she repeated.

And they all slept then, half-waking and sleeping again, half-sleeping, scratching and full of aches and pain. The horse's skin shivered with flies that also bothered Teresa, tickling her face and buzzing in her ear. When the shade from the overhanging rock moved with the sun, the horse moved with it, crowding closer to the tree, his body radiating more heat.

Near dawn, the coolest part of the day, Teresa dreamed she was lying next to a fire. If she didn't push it away, she would burn up. This was worse than the Governor's kitchen, worse than a summer full of baking turkeys and ducks and bread. She pushed out with her hands, strangely unafraid of the red coals or yellow-orange flames. She beat the fire down—and woke to find herself hitting Pomo, shoving him out of the shade and into the sun. The little boy didn't care. He didn't even moan. Shocked, Teresa dragged his body back under the tree. Fever had made his skin hot to touch. He was the fire.

Desperately, Teresa looked about at the horse, at the boulder, at the blue sky. No, no, she thought. She couldn't bear it.

Now someone was coming for her, across the desert, weaving through the needled cactus and mesquite. Someone was shouting her name, "Teresa! Teresa!"

Teresa began to cry silently, for it was her father. The lone figure was Cabeza de Vaca. As the man came closer, she saw that he had aged terribly after his years in the south as the Governor of the Río de la Plata, after his own men of arms had rebelled against him. His beard and hair were completely white, his skin mottled like old leather. Still his pale blue eyes were the same, and his long nose, and most of all, his wonderful voice.

"Teresa!" he called. "I have been looking for you. I have been calling and calling out for you, seeking you wherever I go. Praise the Heavenly Father! I have never been so happy. My greatest wish has come true."

Her father was here at last. She had always known he would come back for her.

"Teresa," he said, and she wanted only to get up and run to him. She wanted only to be held in his arms.

15

"Thank God in His infinite mercy," her father repeated himself. "We have been reunited! How often I have prayed for this day. Come to me, dear child. Dear child!" Cabeza de Vaca opened his arms as he walked toward her. He was dressed as a well-to-do Spaniard, in an embroidered cotton shirt and leather pants, with strong well-made sandals but without the helmet or metal armor of a conquistador. His white beard had been trimmed not long ago although his long white hair flowed freely about his shoulders, having escaped its leather tie. His clothes were stained, as though he had also been walking for miles in the hot desert. Across his shoulder he carried a flat leather bag.

"Teresa, I have looked for you! Oh, so long! You cannot know the countless weeks and months and years I have spent thinking of you and praying for you," her father spoke in his usual voluble fashion. "After those godless colonists turned against me, my own misguided men took me back to Spain, a prisoner in the hold of the ship. A prisoner! Fortunately, the King rallied to my side. After I was vindicated and released, I immediately sailed back to Vera Cruz and took a horse to Mexico City. I am done, finished, with the southern provinces and their ungrateful inhabitants. I rode like a madman to the Governor's house only to find that you were gone and the house deserted. Imagine my feelings! I began to walk north. I knew, yes, somehow I knew I would find you. The Redeemer would help me find you. I had faith, and my faith kept me strong and brought me to you and you to me."

Her father was very close now. Teresa could see the spittle on his beard. She stood up painfully and took a step back into the mesquite tree.

Her father stopped. "Teresa, what is wrong?"

"The boy is sick." She hesitated.

"Sick? You have a sick child? Let me see," her father demanded.

"Stay away!"

"Teresa," her father chided. He held up his hands, palms out. Then he put them together in a gesture of prayer. "Perhaps I can help. I am a healer, after all."

Teresa felt dizzy. It was true. Her father was a healer. She had seen how he had taken the arrowhead from the man's chest, how the man had jumped up the next day completely well. She had seen many other healings as well. Now her father said that he had been looking for her all these months and years. In one soft corner of her hard heart, she had dreamed of this.

"I can see what has happened," her father said briskly. "You are suffering from lack of water and food. You are not thinking clearly. Unfortunately, I used up my own water and food some time ago." He thumped his flat leather bag. "But I recently passed a sizable group of prickly pear cactus. I am afraid the fruits are past their prime. Still, a few are left, juicy and red. I meant to stop and eat them myself. Then I decided—I felt it in the depths of my soul—that something was leading me this way. Let's go there now. Come, come, you can carry the boy."

Teresa bent down and touched Pomo. He was so hot under the cotton shirt. His chest lifted as he breathed in and out with a rasping sound. She cradled him in her arms and picked him up, staggering to her feet. She stepped back again, away from her father.

"Oh, my dearest," he said. "I am so sorry. What has happened to you? You must drink and eat. You must come with me."

Cabeza de Vaca smiled, his teeth still good, his smile so tender that Teresa felt faint. She felt as though her ribs were being squeezed. Her father nodded. "Put the boy on the horse and we will walk there together to the ripe, red prickly pear fruit." Her father turned to Horse and started. "Why, poor animal! He needs nourishment, too. He looks about to expire."

From the corner of her eye, Teresa saw Horse, his head hanging down. She wasn't sure if he knew what was happening. What choice do we have? Teresa thought. If her father were not telling the truth, if there were no prickly pear fruit, then they would all die. But they would die for certain if they stayed here. The boy was so hot. He needed to drink and eat.

"Don't touch him," she warned her father. "Don't come any closer."

She went to the horse and lifted Pomo onto his back. This was difficult because her arms felt so heavy, and her hands trembled. The limp boy almost slid off again, and she had to hold him there, leaning and trembling against the animal's flank. The gelding jerked and flattened his ears.

It's not far, she told the horse. We have to walk, just a bit.

"Let me help," Cabeza de Vaca said and reached out his hand.

Don't let him, Horse exclaimed suddenly.

"No," Teresa murmured.

Her father scowled. "That's enough," he scolded. "I have been patient. But my patience has a limit. I am your father! You are my daughter! We are together again after so many years, and you will behave appropriately."

"No," Teresa meant to say.

133

But "Yes," she said instead because she wanted it so much.

Her father's hand seemed to close around Pomo's arm. He reached up with his other hand as if to shift the boy into a better, more secure position. He patted Horse's neck. He stroked the fine fur. "Very good," he said. Then he led them to the field of prickly pears.

The food revived her, the red pulp filling her with strength and sweetness. She swallowed and the wetness soothed her throat. The fear gnawing in her chest lessened. She was not going to die. She was going to live. Eagerly, she picked an entire cactus clean, eating one, two, three, four of the oblong purple-red fruits, hardly bothering to scrape away the thorns, sucking and spitting out the tiny black seeds. Once she felt stronger, she still wanted to eat. She didn't want to stop.

But she forced herself to turn to the horse and boy, lifting Pomo down and taking him to a patch of shade under a jojoba bush. Automatically, she checked the bush for nuts. A few remained. After settling the boy's limbs, trying to make him comfortable, she went back to the prickly pears and gathered a dozen more fruit, this time trimming off their thorns with a stick and cutting the fruits in half. She gave these to Horse, holding them on her palm like an apple and coaxing him to eat. He resisted the first bite. But after a nibble, tasting the juice, he gobbled down every one, seeds and all, and she had to go back for more. She put this pile on the ground so the horse could feed himself.

For the boy, she squeezed the oblong shapes and let the red liquid dribble into his mouth. Pomo swallowed convulsively and coughed. She squeezed another fruit and another, her hands stained and slimy, until she managed to get a fair amount of juice down his throat and into his stomach.

Then she rested and ate more fruit herself, each one a miracle. She stripped the jojoba nuts from the bush and knotted them into Pomo's cotton shirt, along with the tinderbox. She picked more fruit, half for her and the boy, half for the horse. All the while, her father watched and smiled.

"Excellent," he encouraged her occasionally. "Yes, that's right. Very good."

Teresa noticed that he didn't eat anything himself. He wasn't thirsty or hungry. She hadn't embraced him yet. That impulse had passed. She still felt the longing—to be safe again in her father's strong arms. But she knew these arms were not really strong, and they certainly were not safe. Perhaps it would be like embracing smoke and air. Perhaps Plague could only give the appearance of form.

The fruit had cleared her mind. She had known all along. This could not be her father. She had made a terrible mistake.

Now Cabeza de Vaca stood next to Horse. In his hand, he held a rope that was looped and knotted around the horse's neck. Teresa didn't know when this had happened, when the shape-shifter had created the appearance of a rope that hadn't been there before. She tried to speak to the gelding, but the animal would not listen or answer. His head hung down. His thoughts were muddy, still focused on eating.

Her father looked at her happily. "The fruit is good for you," he said. "But it is not enough. I know of a spring a league away. Put the boy on the horse. We should go while you have the strength to walk."

"You can't have the boy," Teresa said.

Cabeza de Vaca laughed. "I already have him. You gave him the *sarampión* yourself. Remember? You still had the rash, a lovely sprinkle, on your stomach and thighs. I have only waited for the child to become feverish, the first symptom. In a few days, he will have the rash, too. By then, we will have found someone else, another traveler in the desert."

"He was the one you wanted to go with you into the village," Teresa agreed dully. "You will use him to carry the disease."

"He brings it like a gift. I don't need you any longer. In fact, I have no use for you since you no longer carry my little present. Still, you can come with us. I like the company of humans. I like this form, and I can tell you stories, all kinds of stories." Her father laughed again, in a good mood. He kept one hand on the rope and used the other to rub the gelding's neck. The animal shuddered but did not move away.

But this was another trick. Because Teresa knew that Plague did need her. "What if I don't put the boy on the horse?" she asked. "I don't think you can actually do that on your own. I think you are only smoke and air."

Her father shrugged, conceding the point. "Then the boy will die, without water, without more food. You will both die here."

"What if we find this spring ourselves, a league away?"

"You might find it alone," her father nodded, "if you go in the right direction. But you are too weak to carry the boy. Only the horse can do that. And I have the horse. You let me have him."

Horse? Teresa tried again. The gelding blew out his breath and when Teresa glimpsed into his mind, she saw what he saw: not her father, Cabeza de Vaca, but a plain-featured, stub-fingered, stocky Spaniard. It was his old master who held the end of his rope, the man who had trained and groomed him through so many battles and journeys, a man not yet driven mad with grief.

Kro-oak! A raven flapped to the jojoba bush, the branches dipping under its weight. The black head cocked. The dark eye stared. The bird wanted them to leave so it could eat the remaining scraps of fruit. *Kro-aaak*, the raven cawed, and Teresa's mind cleared just a little more.

"Stupid bird," her father sounded displeased.

Pomo was muttering, "I don't want a tortilla! I don't like that!" The little boy pouted, his poor lips cracked and dry. "We are going to a fiesta," he announced, his eyes glittering before he fell back, neck loose and face slack. Teresa decided. They couldn't stay here. She would put the boy on the horse, and they would go to the spring where she would find a way to escape.

"Good girl," her father praised and pretended to give Pomo a gentle touch as he led the horse north.

He talked all the way. Teresa remembered this. Her father had also chattered incessantly, the words pouring out of his mouth and covering her like a shower of petals, like drops of rain, like a dust storm. It was all she could hear, her father's words, all she could see, all she knew. Because this was Plague and not really her father, he talked now of disease: pustules, fevers, and chills.

He told her about *sarampión*. The epidemic of measles had come from the south, swept through the Governor's province and then stopped as people stopped traveling. Commonly the victim had a cough, a runny nose, and an aversion to food. In a week, you would be feverish, and in a few more days, you would have the rash, starting at the hairline and running down the body. Four days before the rash appeared, and four days afterward, a person with *sarampión* could carry it to someone else. You could give the disease away as you give away a cake or a shawl or a rose. Only, in this case, the person giving the gift also got to keep it, at least for a while.

"How can you give away disease?" Teresa asked.

Her father nodded. A good question. "With a touch," Plague said, "with a sigh, with a sneeze. With a song, with a prayer!" He made a little leap, capering in the gravel and sand.

You died of *sarampión* when the disease crept into your lungs, filling them with water. You died of fever, especially when you were young, for young children had the most mag-nificent fevers. You died if you were hungry or sick from some other disease. You died most painfully if your ears began to hurt. More than half the people in the Governor's province had died. More than half the people ahead would die.

"My hard heart protected me," Teresa said, not really to her father but to herself. "Like the Spanish. They have a protection."

Her father nodded. "The Spanish have already survived the *sarampión*. It will not visit you twice."

"And Pomo?" Teresa held her breath, afraid of the answer.

Plague changed the subject, telling her instead about *viruela*, his favorite disease. "This will interest you," he assured her, "for your father knew the man who brought *viruela* to New Spain. Years before he was made captain of the expedition to *La Florida*, Pánfilo de Narváez came with Hernán Cortés and the first conquistadors. In his ship, a black man suffered with smallpox, the sores not yet formed although the man groaned from a headache that seemed to cleave his skull in two and he screamed at the sensation of a knife stabbing his back. He had dreams, too, the wonderful, bloody, extraordinary dreams of *viruela*. Then he felt better, and he went out into this New World, and from him the pestilence spread like light from the sun. The Aztecs called it *hueyzahuatl*. The sores start in the throat and mouth and travel down the face over the body, pimpling, blistering, leaking pus. The skin looks scalded! Some people begin to bleed from every opening— their mouth, their eyes . . ."

Teresa sighed as her father chattered on in his loud voice. He might have been telling her about his childhood in Seville. "And for all this time, these people can give the disease to others, for weeks and weeks, until they die or they recover. Many do recover, perhaps a little pockmarked, perhaps very marked, perhaps blind in one eye."

Walking next to the conquistador, Teresa felt so tired. She could barely keep up even though they were not moving fast, even though Horse plodded slowly through the heat and thorny plants, his breathing harsh. The horizon shimmered with mirages. Anxiously, she kept checking Pomo, who was still extraordinarily hot. The boy moaned in his sleep, his face pressed to the horse's neck.

"How far is the spring?" Teresa asked.

"Not far," her father said.

"Pánfilo de Narváez . . ." Teresa remembered, trying to keep alert, to watch and think. "He abandoned my father. He took the best rowers, the best boat. 'Save yourselves!' he cried. 'I cannot help you!'"

"Yes, that one was quite a fellow."

"There were prophecies," Teresa recited. "There was magic. My father heard the sound of tambourines. In a place called the Bay of Horses, the men killed their mounts and used the flesh to make leather thongs and water bottles. From manes and tails, they braided ropes and rigging. They built five barges and sailed along the coast. Some went mad and jumped into the water."

"Bravo!" her father praised. "Your memory is fantastic."

"Finally, in another terrible storm, a wave took my father's boat and threw it onto a sandy shore, *juego de herradura.*"

"As far as a horseshoe can be tossed," her father said.

"And he is dead now, isn't he?"

"Pánfilo de Narváez? Yes, he died at sea in that rickety barge and all his best rowers with him. One by one they died until he was left alone, the only one left."

"No, my father," Teresa hissed impatiently. The effort hurt her throat, but she continued, "That's how you can use his form, because he is dead like my mother, like Fray Tomás and the pregnant woman."

But Plague waved a languid hand. "Hush. Don't alarm yourself. I told you that death is not necessary, although it is often the case, as often as not. I can go anywhere the disease has gone before me. I know everyone I have ever touched. I knew your father early, when he was a child in Seville, when he had a bad case of *sarampión*. And then later a light case of *viruela*, very light. Then, naturally, he caught the *tabardillo* from all those lice in his clothes on that second trip back to Spain."

"The second trip?"

"As I have already explained to you. After the colonists rebelled against him, they threw him into chains and took him back to the King. Can you imagine? The famous *hidalgo* in chains. His own men testified against him. I don't know how he survived the shame. He never ceases to amaze me. You know, he is an old man now. In truth, he was not so young when he first came to the New World."

The horse snorted, raising his head.

"The animal smells water," Cabeza de Vaca said. "The spring is very close. God has given us this grace and mercy! Blessed Redeemer, thank you!" And Plague knelt mockingly in the sand and gravel, like her father, but not her father.

16

Teresa drank and tended to Pomo, fixing a bed for him by the spring with a hackberry tree for shade. She brought him water in her cupped hands and bathed his body, using the cotton shirt as a cloth. His skin was blotched with heat and abrasions from riding the horse, and his arms and legs were thin and frail. Now he looked like any starving Indian slave. But the fever, Teresa thought, was not worse. The boy even opened his eyes and recognized her.

"Eat," she said, offering him the remaining jojoba nuts.

Pomo turned his face away.

"I can't believe this," Teresa tried to joke. "You're not hungry?"

Fortunately, they had hours before sunset, and she determined she would catch some meat—a rabbit or lizard—and cook a broth the boy could swallow. She looked over at Plague, who held the rope looped around Horse's neck as the animal grazed. Her father smiled back at her. "Drink and we will walk on!" he said jauntily.

"No," Teresa protested, "we have to rest for the night." Of course, she thought, he was in a hurry to reach the next village. He only had a few days while Pomo still had the rash, still carried the *sarampión*. "The boy has to rest," she said, "or he will die. You don't want that."

Her father frowned and seemed inclined to argue. Teresa tried to speak to Horse. But the animal still seemed dazed. She reached into the horse's mind, felt the dark smoke, and quickly withdrew.

"What is my father doing in Spain?" she asked to distract Plague, going closer to the spring and squatting there. Now Plague told her about her father's wife, how kind she was and beautiful and loving. This wife's wealth had allowed Cabeza de Vaca to go to the New World as treasurer of the Pánfilo de Narváez expedition, and while he was gone those eight long years, this loving wife had remained steadfast, raising their two sons with the expectation that their father would return to them. When he did return, he was the best of husbands, writing his report to the King of Spain, until the day he announced that he wanted to sail again across the ocean as Governor of the Río de la Plata, all the way to the Straits of Magellan. With the patience of a saint, this glorious wife used her influence on the King and waved fondly as her husband left again. With the patience of the Redeemer Himself, she welcomed him back after his second disastrous trip, when he was now a criminal accused of treason.

Plague gestured as if with indignation. The enemies of Cabeza de Vaca claimed that he had denied the colonists their lawful rights, stolen money, angered the Indians, and defied the King. None of it was true! The accusations came from greedy men who only wanted to exploit the Indians and keep all the rewards of the New World for themselves. At this very moment, the aging conquistador was under house arrest in his home, busy proving himself innocent. He signed documents and wrote letters all morning, during which time he also discussed his affairs with his two grown sons, prepared his lawyers, and sent them to court with sonorous words ringing in their ears. In the afternoon, he found time to play with his charming grandchildren. In the evening, there were guests, dinner parties, and amusing events.

Teresa listened and tried to imagine her father's new life. She saw the red bougainvillea in the tiled courtyard, the beautiful Spanish wife sitting beside her husband, the bustle of servants in the background. Her father's two daughters-in-law wore magnificent dresses over crinkled underskirts. Their dark hair glittered with jeweled pins. Her father complimented a particular necklace. They praised his recent discussion of reform in the West Indies. Oh yes, her father assured them, he believed in Spain's divine mission and right to ownership of these lands and to all the people in them. But he also believed that the natives of the New World had souls and that these souls could be brought to Christendom with gentleness and kindness. He referred his daughters-in-law to the teachings of the Greeks. He quoted a rhyme in Latin, and they murmured appreciatively.

Teresa studied the women sitting around the table. She looked everywhere, but she could not see herself in this courtyard. She did not sit by the saint-like wife or one of the beautiful daughters-in-law. She was not listening and smiling, dressed in a magnificent skirt with her hair lifted to cover the flattened back of her head. She did not gossip with her sisters, discussing their children and the upcoming fiesta, occasionally touching the four blue tattoos on each cheek. She was not in the background, either, as a servant. Her father did not catch her eye as she gave him his sweetened drink or hurried by with a broom or feather duster. She was simply not there. She had no place.

She didn't really care. What Teresa wanted now was to stone a rabbit. She wanted Plague to stop talking so she could hunt for Pomo's supper, and for her own, before it was dark. She wanted to poke around the nearby bushes, look for a pack-rat's nest or the roots of nut-grass or some other edible plant. How fortunate that I still have the tinderbox, Teresa thought for the hundredth time. It would be so nice to build a fire and

143

cook some meat, to smell it roasting, to make a nourishing meal for Pomo.

"Your father is certain he will win his case," Plague rambled on. "He is certain he will be granted his old titles of land in Spain and even reimbursed for his lost estates near the Río de la Plata. He is seeking compensation for his services to various municipal courts and once these ridiculous charges are dismissed . . ."

"You say he is old now?" Teresa interrupted.

"He walks with a cane. He has the voice of an old man."

She rose, brushing the dirt from her leather skirt. "What about Pomo?" she tried to surprise Plague. "Will he survive the *sarampión*?"

Her father's eyes twinkled, and he wagged his finger. "Ah, ah, ah! I can't say for sure." And before he could drone on again, about his estates and the King, Teresa announced that she had to find food, if only a few nuts or pieces of root, a grasshopper or worm. She left Plague still talking to himself.

Soon after, a hare came to drink from the spring, and she killed it quickly, hacked it apart with a sharp rock, built a fire, skewered and roasted the carcass, and mixed its juices with water in the indentation of a large flat boulder on which, she thought, she could also sit and perhaps later grind seeds or nuts. She drizzled this soup into Pomo's mouth, although he twisted and tried to turn away. Then with her own stomach full, in the growing darkness, she thought about what she should do next. She wished she could ask Horse's advice.

Close by, her father watched, still holding on to the rope. "Shall I tell you about my estates in . . ."

"No," Teresa said, "I have to sleep."

For breakfast the next morning, she drank water and gnawed the bones clean, giving Pomo the rest of the soup. Sitting beside the boy, she chipped at the edges of her sharp rock, making a new cutting tool to replace the one she had left behind. In the distance, she could see agave stalks, the single spire rising up like a yucca with a similar base of thick pointed leaves. She knew it was possible to bake and eat agave root, although it would be hard work digging up the sturdy plant. She wondered if there was enough grass here for Horse. She hoped so.

"Come on," her father clapped his hands. "You have had your rest, and it is time to go. Put the boy on the horse."

Teresa sat where she was, still flinting and hoping she could actually make this tool into a real knife. "No," she said. "We are staying here."

Oh, her father shouted and protested, stomped and stormed, but it was as she had thought. Plague couldn't do much on his own. He could assume a shape that looked solid. He could cloud the mind of a horse and guide its movements. He could talk for hours. He could wheedle and coax and threaten. But she hadn't seen him yet make a physical action—kick a rock or eat a prickly pear or pick up a boy. He could not lift Pomo onto the horse's back. He could not take Pomo away from her.

"We will take our chances in the desert," she informed her father. "We have water now. I can find food. Pomo will recover, and then we will go on."

"Nonsense," Plague huffed. She felt a cloud enter her mind. Dark smoke. *Fear.*

She brushed it away.

17

Teresa felt good. The more Cabeza de Vaca begged, the better she felt. This was the right decision. Pomo seemed better this morning, too. He didn't feel so hot. The boy would get well, and Plague would have no need for him.

Plague threatened, "I'll leave with the horse."

"Go on, then." Teresa called his bluff. A horse could not help him enter the next village with the disease. He needed a human being. "Once Pomo is well," she repeated, "we can go on alone without Horse." She kept her face impassive, her voice steady. She couldn't let Plague know how much she cared about the animal.

"Daughter!" her father said.

Teresa laughed. "You are not my father. You told me so yourself."

The conquistador disappeared and rearranged himself into a pillar of smoke. The gelding snorted with terror. Teresa took a deep breath, calming herself before she spoke. "That won't work either." Deliberately, she turned her attention back to Pomo, feeling his forehead and wetting his face.

Fray Tomás reappeared, still holding on to Horse's rope.

"Oh, stop it!" Teresa scoffed and felt clever. She had out-witted Plague.

But her triumph was short-lived. Naturally she had noticed prints in the dirt around the spring, human footprints and animal tracks, deer and peccary, mice and rabbit. Everyone in the desert came here to drink, and anyone walking from the nearest villages would know this place. It was sheer bad luck—although not unusual—that two hunters came to the spring that very afternoon. Summer was the season of prickly pear fruit. If you had a gourd or leather bag for your water, this was a good time to get away from wives and chores and the domestic life of the village.

The two hunters approached without guile. At this time of day, they did not expect to see any game, and so they did not hide or sneak up to the spring. Teresa saw them before they saw her and crept out from under the shade of the hackberry tree where she rested with Pomo. She had to warn the men away—but how? Standing up in plain sight, she pushed the backs of her hands away in a flapping movement. Shoo, shoo. That was what the cooks did in the Governor's kitchen to scatter the geese and turkeys crowding around the door. Shoo. Shoo. She hoped these hunters would understand. Go away, her hands signaled. Go away!

The men wore cotton loincloths and cotton shirts, with bags and gourds slung over their shoulders. Each also carried a bow. They paused when they saw her and conferred together.

Teresa tried shouting, "A boy here has the gift of *sarampión*. You will be safe if you go quickly!" She hoped they understood Spanish.

But the hunters were gesturing at something behind Teresa on the other side of the spring, and as Teresa turned to look, she knew what she would find. Her father was gone. A stranger stood beside Horse and held the rope attached to the gelding's neck. Like the two men, this man was short and stocky, dressed in a cotton loincloth and cotton shirt. His wrinkled face was also clean-shaven, and he spoke now—yelling through cupped hands—in a language the others recognized. They shouted in reply and nodded and came closer. They looked surprised but also pleased, exclaiming loudly and even smacking their lips over the horse.

"No, don't!" Teresa tried to warn them.

The third man spoke again, pointing at her and shaking his head, gesturing. The three men talked for a short time, probably in Opata, for all this country belonged to the Opata people, who used irrigation to grow maize and beans and who built grand houses of stone and adobe. To the north and east, their villages dotted the edge of the desert. Teresa had long assumed the wise woman was an Opata, too.

Teresa knew how convincing Plague could be. His manner was earnest, his voice urgent. Clearly he was an elder, a respected man from a village these hunters had probably never visited before—a village, Teresa thought, who had felt the wing brush of death for Plague to have assumed this man's shape. These hunters had no reason to doubt such a man. They had no reason to refuse him.

They moved toward Teresa with obvious intent. She wished suddenly for the black Moor who had seemed to know every language in the world. She berated herself for speaking only Spanish. There had been Opatas serving in the Governor's house. Opatas and Jumanos and Aztecs and Mayans. But she had never bothered to learn their speech. She had never cared what anyone else was saying.

One of the men bent over Pomo. "Don't touch him!" Teresa tried to wrench the man's arm away. He pushed her aside, but still she beat at his shoulders and head as he lifted the boy. Pomo cried out, waking from his sleep. As Teresa ran after them, the other hunter grabbed her, roughly pulling her elbows back. She gasped with the pain. These were strong hunters. They were much stronger than she was. There was nothing she could do.

Plague echoed her thoughts, addressing her in Spanish, "Stop getting in the way. There is nothing you can do."

Teresa dangled from the hunter's grip. He shook her and then pushed her to the ground. She moved away from him, creeping backward toward the hackberry tree, the empty place where Pomo had been just a moment ago.

"Don't take him to your village," she begged the man, but he only stared at her and touched his face. Her blue tattoos had made him curious. He tapped his cheek and wrinkled his nose as if to say, "How ugly!"

"Don't try to come with us," Plague said to Teresa, again in Spanish. "I have explained to them that you are a bad person, a witch who has stolen this boy from his rightful parents. I told them how you poisoned the child, how you want to drink his blood to feed your power. Since you speak Spanish, I told you were a Christian witch, and they are properly impressed and horrified. Don't follow us now. If you do, I will tell them to kill you."

By now, Pomo lay slumped on Horse's back. The Opata made another speech, and both hunters went to the spring to drink and fill their gourds and leather pouches. Then they trotted off obediently, leading the way back to their village. It was the direction they had come from and probably not the way they had meant to go next. Still, they seemed content to do what the elder told them to do.

"Stop, please!" Teresa had to call out one more time. She dropped to her knees.

The Opatas never looked back. But Plague turned to face her, and as he did, he changed again from an older Opata man dressed in cotton shirt and loincloth to a much older Opata woman in a leather skirt, her bone-white hair braided down her back, her breasts bare but for a seashell necklace.

The wise woman smiled, and Teresa could hear Plague whispering, not out loud but in her thoughts. Remember me?

Remember how I came to you in the barn where you shivered with chills and burned with fever? I walked with you out of the Governor's house through the village. I hurried you north. I drove you north, faster and faster.

Teresa was glad she was already on her knees. What a fool she was. An ignorant servant girl. An ignoble bastard. Tricked from the beginning. Years ago, the wise woman had looked straight at Cabeza de Vaca, never at her. *What you have lost will be restored to you.* And so it had been. So her father had returned to Spain, to his wife, to his King.

And the real wise woman?

Dead, Plague told her. Dead from the *sarampión,* which kills, most especially, the very young and very old.

Now Plague was turning and taking Horse with him, taking away Pomo. It had all happened so quickly. It was over so quickly. Teresa was dumbfounded. Pomo looked small and unresisting slung over the horse's back like a captured animal. And Horse, too. The Opatas had smacked their lips as you do over a pile of meat or berries or other good food. They were leading him back to the village to butcher. They were thinking about their next feast and dance.

Teresa let herself collapse onto the ground, onto the hard dirt, her mouth tasting dirt, dirt filling her eyes. There was nothing she could do, nowhere she could go, no one who could help her. She should just die here. She should lie here in the hot sun and never get up. She should let her body feed the coyotes and ravens. Almost, Teresa felt pleased about this decision. She was tired of being so empty and unhappy.

A movement swelled, pushing gently against her stomach.

What? Her stomach asked.

Teresa tried to listen. Since leaving the Governor's house, not even a month ago, a matter of weeks, she had found herself speaking to Horse and to the jaguar. But that was not the same as speaking to the earth. *That* had been so very long ago. She could hardly remember. She had stopped asking, stopped caring.

Do you still love me? she whispered now.

What you have lost will be restored to you.

I need your help.

I am all alone.

I don't know what to do.

Teresa understood she had to be patient. She spread her arms as though embracing all the flatness of the desert. She turned so that her cheek pressed into soil, gravel and leaves and prickly thorns. In the distance she could see the green edge of the spring and a patch of blue sky. She was prepared to wait for as long as necessary. This was her last hope to save Pomo and Horse. She closed her eyes. She was prepared to wait like this for hours.

Of course, I love you, the earth said, rippling with amusement. Why would I not love you?

The voice was so familiar. I have been away, Teresa replied, ashamed.

Have you? The earth was curious. Where have you been?

Teresa thought. For a moment, she couldn't remember. With my father, she answered at last. With the housekeeper in the Governor's kitchen, with Fray Tomás. With the horse. And the boy.

Tell me a secret, the earth said. Tell me a secret about *me*.

The earth was growing softer, softer, and her body fitted so easily into its curves.

I have to tell you about Plague first. I need your help.

I know Plague, the earth said, uninterested.

Then you've seen the villages! Teresa exclaimed. You've seen the people crying and moaning. You've seen how the mothers and fathers cry when their children suffer. You know about the sores and scalded skin, the smell of bodies. You've heard the silence.

Yes, the earth said. I like watching people. I like watching what you do.

But how can we stop him? Teresa asked, meaning the form of Plague that had tricked and chased and brought her here.

Why should we stop him? the earth wondered.

Listen to me, Teresa said. She tried to explain how the pockmarked housekeeper had loved life. That strong busy woman had loved to eat and make good food. She had loved to feed people. She had loved to stand in the kitchen before all her cooks and assistant cooks and assistants to the assistant cooks as they chopped and cut and pounded and stirred. Teresa felt a pang. The housekeeper was dead, and Teresa had not even tried to help her or say good-bye. She tried to explain to the earth how the women in the kitchen had sung so bravely, so afraid but still cheerful, still singing and gossiping. She tried to make the earth see how Fray Tomás had taught the Indian boys and girls to read, how he had patted Teresa's hair, how he had nursed the sick. She remembered the horse's master who had gone insane mourning his wife, wrapping their dead child into her arms. She described the bleeding heart of Christ, how a man nailed to a cross could feel compassion for all the world, for all the suffering people.

The earth shrugged. They will come back to me, the earth reminded her. I will still love them.

Yes, but . . . Teresa wished she had the words. She wished she could speak like her father with all his words.

I want Pomo, she said at last. Help me find Pomo. Please.

The earth hemmed and hawed.

Please, Teresa coaxed, and let herself sink deeper. Long ago, she had felt the excitement in her veins and watched the magic crackle from her father into yucca and saltbush and locust tree. Long ago, her foster mother had said she would be a woman of power. Long ago, she had floated toward the rattling pebbles in the gourd. Now was the time. If she were ever to find and use that power . . . Teresa gathered herself and let herself sink deeper, her arms stretching and reaching out. She bent her neck and fell forward, downward. She felt the earth soften. She remembered the girl with long black hair who could swim through rivers of stone. That girl had moved through stone as easily as the wind moves through the branches of a tree. This is how it feels! Teresa thought. Her feet and legs, her groin, her stomach, her breasts, her hands, her arms and shoulders, her face settled more deeply into the softening ground. She was about to disappear.

Only something held her back. Something hard and unyielding. Teresa felt her ribs enter the earth and then stop, unable to go further. It was her hard heart. Her hard heart could not come with her. For a second, Teresa hesitated. She needed that protection against disease—against memories. She thought of her father in his courtyard in Spain, scratching at his papers, playing with his grandchildren. He had conquered the New World, and now he wanted his estates back. He had wrapped her in his arms and in his language, whispering about a life she did not understand although understanding seemed to form just beyond the sea and sand, waiting there for her to grow older. Even when the story confused her, she had caught words or phrases, ideas like fish, bold and surprising, tasting of her father's mind. She had learned quickly to nod and speak because he needed her to do this, because his need surrounded her like the blue sky. She was his bastard, and he had loved her. Yes, he had loved her. That was the memory she couldn't bear. He had loved her, and he had lifted her up from the bed of crushed oyster shells away from her familiar life. He had taken her on his journey, and nothing had ever been the same.

For the first time, Teresa wondered . . . if this were such a bad thing. Did she wish to have been left behind with her tribe, dying later with her mother and aunts and baby sister? Would she choose now not to have met the Moor or Fray

153

Tomás or the housekeeper? Or Horse or Pomo? Should her father have taken her with him to Spain? Or had Dorantes been right? Would the Inquisition have burned them as they burned so many others?

And did any of that matter now? If her hard heart would not let her enter the earth, then she would leave that anger behind. She was her father's daughter, practical and determined. She had not come this far to be stopped so easily.

So easily, then, Teresa sank into the ground until the ground closed over her shoulders and rump and the backs of her legs, her leather skirt left behind, her yucca sandals and a strange twisted knot of dark-red stone, something for an Opata villager to puzzle over when he found her clothes and took them as a prize, something for someone many years later to look at and pick up and toss aside.

Teresa reached out with her arms and parted the earth, kicking her legs as if swimming through the salty bay where she was born, until she glided into a bed of white and gray granite. Glittering pieces of quartz flashed like fireflies. By the light of this rock, she could see her hands flashing in front of her, too, as she propelled herself forward. Now she gave her heels another kick, swimming slightly upward and then straight ahead, parallel to the desert floor above. She knew that Pomo and Horse and Plague and the two Opata hunters had gone in this direction, for she could scent them, following their trail as a mountain lion might follow a deer through grass. She hunted the hunters, rippling under their feet.

All around her, the earth seemed pleased, like a child who has convinced an adult to come play.

18

It was hard to keep track of time. Teresa swam through white granite with flashing crystals: quartz, mica, feldspar. Sometimes the air was tinged pink, and sometimes it darkened to light gray, but she could always see far enough ahead to feel comfortable, as though she were swimming through the water of a mostly clear pond. She had no fear of bumping into anything, for she glided through rocks of every size and texture. Nothing, really, was in her way.

Above her on the desert floor, light exploded and shimmered over the dry land. There the hard rock would bruise her body, the cactus thorns make her bleed, the sun burn her exposed skin. In that distant difficult world, Horse plodded across the sand with Pomo slumped on his back and Plague by his side holding the end of a frayed rope. The two Opata hunters led the way. They walked carelessly. They felt important. Each step brought disaster closer to their village.

When she concentrated, Teresa could hear those steps, the sound of horse hooves and sandaled feet reverberating through the earth. Once she found this small group, she kept pace with them, following behind and stopping when they stopped—which was not often. The Opatas were used to running all day. Teresa imagined how they had to force poor exhausted Horse, scolding in his ear, slapping his flank, only occasionally giving him sips of water from their cupped hands. She knew that Plague would stand aside then, pretending to busy himself with some other concern.

She did not know any of this for a fact. She could not really see what the Opata hunters were doing. She did not know if Pomo looked better or worse. She wasn't there when Horse stumbled or the boy cried out. She wondered if the shapeshifter Plague bothered even to leave fake footprints, or if he walked like a ghost and the hunters were too stupid to notice.

The bed of granite curved in another direction, and Teresa moved now through hardened river sand, ripples of deposited brown, orange, and yellow. It was hard to keep track of time, but when Horse and the Opatas stopped moving and did not move again even as many minutes seemed to pass, Teresa guessed that it was night. They had been traveling all day. Now they slept.

She did not feel the need to sleep. She explored a nearby field of red and purple rock. The rock barely remembered its fiery past, the day it shot molten from the center of the earth, flowing over trees and bushes and hissing into the shallow water of a broad lake. Eventually, the lake dried and rivers came from the north bringing sand and gravel, and those layers hardened, and now the rock drowsed under their weight, happy to be hidden again.

Teresa examined herself, her arms and legs, five fingers on each hand, five toes on each foot. Her flesh seemed exactly the same to her. She could grasp her nose. She could tug her hair. Her skin was soft. What was different?

For one thing, she had traveled all day without feeling hungry or thirsty or tired. Also, she noticed, her chest did not rise up and down with each breath. In fact, she was not breathing. She no longer needed air.

I am feeding you, the earth whispered. The voice came from all around, top and bottom, every side, everywhere. You are drinking from me. Your food comes from me.

I am no longer . . . human? Teresa asked.

The earth had to think about this.

You are human, the earth said finally, for I can feel you aging. I can feel your body changing in human time, not the time I know. Definitely, you are human. You could grow old here. You could die here. The earth sounded hopeful, as if this would be a good idea. I have so much to show you, the earth said.

Yes, Teresa agreed, but only while they are sleeping.

She followed the earth's echoing call, here, here, here, across the field of red and purple rock to a limestone reef where she swam through the plants and animals of the sea, through curved shells, bony fish, and the long skeletons of monsters with pointed teeth and flippers and tails. She passed through the imprint of many-fingered kelp, and then through a forest of kelp taller than the tallest cactus, the tall plants seeming to sway rhythmically with the tide. She heard the drumming of waves in stone.

Here, here, here! the earth cried with excitement, and now Teresa dove through the jaws of a predator for whom she would have been a bite and a snap. The creature's power and menace still felt palpable, his thigh bones massive for the muscled strength with which he ran down his prey, his upper arms short with two claws on each hand for grabbing and seizing and tearing apart. Teresa got a glimpse of small gleaming eyes, still bright in the bones of his skull, and she shivered as she swam in and out of his ribs.

Is this where he lived? she asked. Here with you?

Oh, no, the earth answered. He lived with the others. And the earth told her about the fast-moving, egg-laying, gigantic creatures that had crashed through the vines and bushes and trees in the wet steamy jungle above, stalking each other, eating each other, whipping their enormous tails, mating ferociously, grazing in herds that stretched for leagues. They could make extraordinary sounds, hooting and whistling.

They had tails and laid eggs? Teresa marveled. She thought of how lizards could move fast to dart under rocks and the roots of trees. In winter, they slowed down, hiding in their burrows.

But no, the earth smiled, remembering. These animals never slowed down. They were always passionate. They had such strong emotions! I always wondered what they would do next.

Teresa walked across a hardened lake bed. She had discovered that she could walk and run as well as swim. She could somersault and cartwheel. She could jump and leap and come to a stop. At the same time, she could also choose to sink into the very lake she was walking across, falling downward, drifting slowly or turning around headfirst and plummeting fast. She could stand, flap her arms like a bird, and fly up into a sky of stone. She could go wherever she wanted.

One day, the earth continued its story, a change swept over the surface of the land. A wave passed through the hills and mountains. The ground shuddered, and the oceans roiled. After that, the giant creatures were gone. The earth rose up to cover some of them, like this one here, while the others broke apart into dust. Now in that steamy world, the small mammals that had lived under the giants' feet grew bigger, more passionate themselves, more full of life until they roamed the grassland where the jungle had been.

Teresa thought of the turtle shaking off its burden of people. The world did not end. But it changed.

It is changing, the earth agreed.

Teresa thought of Plague. The empty villages and the shapeshifters, slaves now, dying of disease, so many people dying, a wave of change sweeping over the landscape. Horse and Pomo.

Pomo! Teresa thought. Although time seemed to pass in the usual way, it was hard to remember its passing, to remember or care about day or night on the surface above. Suddenly she wondered how many hours had gone by while she played, distracted, among the bones of monsters and forests of kelp. In the desert above, the bright sun might be high now, the morning come and gone—with Plague always hurrying the Opatas, anxious to reach their village.

Quickly, she swam upward and then sideways, casting for the sound of footprints. At last, she heard them and listened more closely. Something was wrong. Someone was missing. The horse's step was too light.

Where was Pomo? Furious at herself, she backtracked, listening hard for the beating of a small boy's heart, the pulse of blood in his feet where his feet touched the ground. When she heard that faint *thump, thump,* she felt further alarmed, for Pomo's heartbeat was so weak. His heartbeat was like the end of a song, the last notes fading into silence.

In a panic, she rose up—half out of the earth, half in the earth.

On a stretch of white sand, Pomo lay on his side, barely breathing. He lay in the sun with no protection, no cotton shirt, no water or food, no one to take care of him. All along his naked body, Teresa could see the rash of *sarampión,* small red dots filling with pus. Soon they would crust and dry and fall away. She suspected that the boy's fever had broken and the disease was no longer a threat to his life. Now it was the desert, the sun and heat, that would kill him. Quickly she spread her hands over the boy's face, splaying her fingers to provide some shade. But she had nothing else to give, no way to help. It would not take long for the vultures to begin circling the sky.

Why had they left him so unprotected? Teresa could only imagine the scene. Waking in the early light, lifting the unconscious boy onto the horse, the Opatas had finally seen the rash spread over the child's skin. This boy was sick, not poisoned! The Christian witch had infected the boy! Oh, the hunters had heard of this illness, the fever burning and the rash spreading and all the children dying and many adults, too. Reasonably now, they did not want to bring a sick child into their village. That was no cause for celebration. Reasonably, they wanted to abandon Pomo here without further thought, without food or water—for that would be an act of mercy. The boy should die as quickly as possible. Reasonably, Plague did not object. Perhaps Plague had even encouraged this idea. The gift was given. Now the Opatas carried the gift in their bodies. Plague didn't need Pomo anymore.

Still half in the earth, Teresa looked about, straining to see something that would help the boy—a jojoba bush, a tall-limbed cactus. The air was so heavy, the ground was so hot, the sun was so bright.

It was different in the earth. There she felt light, weightless, neither hot nor cold. Her hard heart had been left behind, and her new old heart beat just as well, just as strongly. There the light was dim and nourishing. The earth fed her and gave her its energy. The earth loved and protected her.

Without thinking, Teresa reached out and took Pomo and pulled him to her chest. She felt the comfort of his body. Then she sank back into the rivers of stone.

Pomo woke at the shock, and he was afraid. He wiggled against Teresa as she turned and kicked and propelled them downward with one arm. Holding him more firmly with both hands, she wasn't sure at first how to move through the earth. Then she found herself pushing forward with the top of her head—a wrinkling of her brow, a determined thought. She pushed forward and glided. This was easier when she followed the veins of certain minerals running through the rock beds, as though these shining threads had already created movement. She pushed with the top of her head. She glided. She followed a streak of copper that chimed like the bells her father had once prized.

But Pomo continued to kick and scream with more strength than Teresa would have imagined in a sick child. "Stop it!" she scolded, struggling to hold on to the thrashing boy. "It's all right. You're all right now!" She didn't know if she spoke these words out loud or silently. In any case, Pomo ignored her, thinking himself in the grip of another dream, in the clutches of Plague. He twisted and turned, trying to escape, trying to bite her.

He does not belong here, the earth said. Put him to sleep.

That's a good idea, Teresa replied as Pomo's elbow punched her in the stomach. It was like holding a big slippery fish with teeth and nails. His skinny body bucked. His feet churned. How do I do that? Teresa asked, doubling over to catch Pomo before he fell.

Just do it, the earth said. So she did.

The boy's body loosened. Teresa held him tight again and felt relieved and then anxious. She checked him quickly. Of course, he wasn't breathing, and his eyes were closed, long lashes against the smooth cheek. But his face looked peaceful, and she felt the life, the warm blood flowing under his skin. She rested his body against her hip as she swam one-handed to a red rock slab rising up through lighter layers of sand. There she lay the boy down as though she were laying him on a bed in the Governor's house—although in truth she had no idea of up or down anymore—and there she slowly took her hands away, glad to see he did not sink further into rock. His eyelids flickered. He drank from the earth. He fed from the earth.

All the while, the disease would run its course. Although the fever was gone, the rash still had to heal, and the sores melt away. Meanwhile, Teresa only had to wait until Pomo got better and they could return to the surface and continue their journey.

She wondered where they would go now that the wise woman was dead. Or had that been another trick? How could she believe anything Plague told her?

And what about Horse? Plague and Horse and the Opatas were walking on now, closer to the Opata village. Teresa thought of how the hunters would return home triumphantly, how the women and children would rush forward to greet them. Everyone would be exclaiming. "Look, a horse!" "Look, here is an elder from another village!" "What good fortune!" "How lucky we are!" "Welcome, welcome!"

Plague would smile charmingly. The villagers would kill Horse so that everyone could eat meat, and they would dance before a bonfire and drink yellow tea. Teresa imagined a young girl leaning against one of the hunter's legs. "Have you brought me a gift?" the child asked. The Opata brought his face down to hers.

Teresa straightened, decided, looked down at Pomo, and spoke to the earth: will you watch over him? Will you keep him safe?

It has been a long time, the earth said, since someone like you has come to visit me.

Does that mean yes? Teresa asked.

The earth rippled with amusement.

19

Teresa rose up again toward the surface, the hot desert floor. Again she listened for the footsteps of the two Opata hunters, the hard hooves of the gelding. She glided back and forth underground, straining to hear and understand what she was hearing. There, yes. That was Horse. And there were the two hunters, walking faster now, for they had used up all their water and food and didn't want to spend another night in the desert. They wanted to reach the village by dark.

Teresa had to think about what to do. Under the Opatas' quickening feet, she glided and hovered and plotted, not wanting to get too far ahead or too far behind. The hunters had to be in the exact right place. She had to do this exactly right.

Finally they were where she wanted them to be—where two monstrous slabs of rock almost-rubbed against each other, where the almost-shuddering space ran just below the surface of the ground. Here in this gap, the two parts longed to touch and did not dare touch. The two parts created a tension, a pulling back and forth. What did these great slabs of rock want? What was pushing them away? What was pushing them together? Questions had gathered. The rocks almost-shuddered with energy. They were almost-alive with energy. They shouted over and over in their great rock voice: What Should We Do?

And Teresa put her mouth to the almost-shuddering slabs of rock and told them what to do. Move, she said.

The rocks were still, as always, and then they moved. One slab buckled sideways. The other slab crushed against it, grinding in the opposite direction. The energy was released. The questions met, and the gap closed, sending a wave of excitement in every direction. For a second, the rocks *were* alive, a second of explosive joy, and then they were rock again.

Teresa flew up to the surface, where everything had occurred in the best possible way—as much as she had dared to hope. In the earthquake, the two Opatas had been thrown to the ground. One was unconscious with a bloodied head. The other looked dazed, half-sitting. A crack had opened next to him, a jagged dividing line, the Opatas on one side and Plague and Horse on the other.

Teresa came partly out of the earth, near where the hunters lay in shock and pain. Run, she told Horse. Can you run away?

The gelding was badly frightened, and his front legs reared. Plague looked startled, too, barely holding on to the end of the rope. With satisfaction, Teresa saw Horse jerk so violently now that Plague lost control of him. The horse rose up again on his back legs, wheeling and turning. Run! Teresa shouted. Run, run! Her voice seemed to energize the animal further, and he galloped away for his very life. Every step weakened Plague's power over him. With every step, the animal grew stronger, and his mind cleared.

Meanwhile Teresa grabbed the hand of one unconscious Opata and the hand of the other dazed Opata and pulled at them as hard as she could. Determined, unstoppable, she dove back into the earth, dragging the two men behind her, willing the top of her head to propel her forward. She streaked down like a comet, using the weight of the two Opatas, adding them to the force and speed of her descent.

Almost immediately, she passed the fault line where the slabs of rock had touched each other. The moment of explosive joy was over. The questions would gather again. What Should We Do? Where Should We Go? The energy would build and the tension and the almost-shuddering.

Teresa plunged, dropped, dove. When the Opata hunter who was still conscious began to scream, she put him to sleep. Then she put the other one to sleep, too, deeper than a knock on the head. She passed through blurs of granite and limestone, layers of sand and silt, veins of copper, veins of gold. She passed them so quickly she couldn't hear them singing. This time, she thought, it was true. This time, she would succeed. This time, she was really outrunning Plague!

At last, when she felt she had gone far enough, Teresa slowed and tried to catch her breath. Of course, she had no breath to catch, but it felt as though she did. Her heart raced. She could feel its pounding. She gripped the hands of the two hunters. She had seen Horse run away. She had left Plague behind.

Very interesting, the earth said.

Is *he* coming after us? Teresa asked.

I don't think so, the earth said. I think *he* is quite confused.

Teresa made a camp in the earth, somewhat like a camp she might make on its surface—only she had no need here for fire or food or water or grass for a bed. Only there were no stars at night, no sun or shade, no breeze, and no real change in the white light of hardened river sand or the purple glow of volcanic rock. She put the two Opata hunters off to the side, a good distance from her and Pomo, where she could still see them. Like Pomo, they seemed to be resting comfortably, their eyes closed, their faces peaceful. After a while, she stopped worrying that they or the boy would sink further into the earth, even though she herself could still go down as far as she wanted.

Now she had many more days to wait, for she could not bring the Opatas back to their village until they no longer carried the disease. She remembered well what Plague had told her. Four days before the rash appeared, and four days afterward, a person with measles could give the disease away as you give away a shawl or cooking pot. She had done this to Pomo when her stomach and groin were still speckled, a few days after her fever broke. Then Pomo had carried the gift to the hunters. Now she had to be patient until the *sarampión* raged through their bodies and was finally gone.

She wondered if she should wake Pomo or let him sleep. She asked the earth.

Let him sleep, the earth said.

But I could show him the animals, Teresa argued. He would like the giant creature with his sharp teeth and still-bright eyes. He would like swimming through the forest of kelp. He would . . .

He does not belong here, the earth interrupted. This is not his power.

After that, Teresa did not like to leave the boy for long, not knowing what would happen if he woke by accident and found himself alone. Because of this, she explored mostly what was around her camp and did not venture on longer trips, not back to the skeletons in the limestone bed or down to where the earth burned with rivers of fire. Longingly, Teresa thought about those rivers with their glimmering darting schools of fish, red and yellow, gold and green—but she would not risk losing Pomo now. They had gone through too much together. She had exposed the boy to disease, given the horse to Plague, and left Pomo in the desert to die. She would not be so careless again. She would only take short walks, not far from the slab of purple rock.

Once when she came back from such a walk, Pomo was gone. In the boy's place, the spotted jaguar lay asleep, his paws twitching. Teresa ran to the big cat. No, she thought sternly. Before her eyes, the animal blurred, shifted, and grew smaller. Pomo reappeared, his dark eyelashes curved against his cheek.

I thought the jaguar was gone, Teresa complained to the earth.

Then the boy would be gone, the earth said. They are the same thing.

After this, she stayed even closer to her camp. She felt the calm and boredom of nothing to do, something she hadn't known since she was a child watching her mother pick black-berries. She listened to the hardened sand, the memories of a river rushing to sea. She listened to the volcanic rock, its mem-ories long ago as fire. She listened to the crooning of a seashell, and she thought of the wise woman and her necklace of shell with gleams of coral pink. Often, she and the earth told each other stories. Often, she was the one telling the story, all the stories she had heard in her life, all her father's stories, all the stories in the Governor's kitchen, all the stories by Fray Tomás and even Plague. After she had exhausted these, she went on to make up new ones—for the earth was insatiable. Tell me more, the earth begged.

The earth begged for secrets but did not always share its own. Once, waiting next to Pomo, Teresa saw a brown speck in the distance coming toward her, coming closer and growing bigger until she saw that this was a bear swimming through stone just as she swam through stone, its paws mov-ing effortlessly. This bear was much bigger than the black bears she had seen in the mountains while traveling with her father. Its head and shoulders were as massive as a buffalo's, with a great hump over the neck. Its fur was grizzled silver-gray. Its mouth widened into a kind of grin. Now the bear seemed to see her and veered off, and Teresa felt relieved.

How many others, Teresa wondered, played in the earth?

It was hard to keep track of time. Time passed in the usual way—the Opatas became feverish in their sleep, red spots appeared on their chests and arms, the pustules broke open and scabbed shut—but it was hard to remember how the hours were rushing by. There was never a real day and never a real night, just a seamless stretch of glowing stone.

Finally, at some moment when it was neither day nor night, neither time to eat nor time to sleep, Teresa bent to look at the sleeping hunters. She saw that their skin was clear and unblemished. The scabs had fallen away, leaving only a few scars, here, here, and here. During the earthquake, one of the Opatas had suffered a bloody gash on his head, and that also had healed and left hardly a sign.

She could take them home now.

20

But she did not.

The earth seemed to approve. They are happy where they are, the earth said.

Teresa doubted that the hunters were happy, away from their wives and children, from their village of good food and yellow tea, from the long days of walking quickly through the desert with their knives and bows and arrows, alert in the physical world. That's what made these hunters happy, not lying asleep underground on a slab of purple rock.

This was true of Pomo, as well. Yes, the boy was safe now. He was protected, as he had been when he slept in the jaguar. But she had not wanted that life for him. Despite the dangers he risked, a small boy at the mercy of disease and Spanish slavers, she had wanted Pomo to have his own life. She had wanted to see him building dams in the stream, spinning a whirligig with a crown of daisies on his head, not lying so still and peaceful, never any trouble to anyone.

Teresa knew she should take the hunters and Pomo back to the world above where the wind blew and the sun shone and the stars glittered in the evening sky. She should leave herself.

But she did not.

Instead, she dithered. She made excuses. It was hard to keep track of time.

Finally one day or maybe one night, she saw another speck in the distance coming closer toward her. The closer the speck came, the bigger it grew, although this animal was hardly as big as a grizzly bear. Nor did it swerve to the side as it got near but kept coming directly at her, seeming to aim and swoop right for her head. Teresa ducked. The big raven croaked and flapped black wings and settled onto the purple rock where Pomo slept quietly.

The raven *kro-oaked* and waddled back and forth in that ungainly way that ravens have when walking instead of flying. *Tlok-tlok-tlok.* The bird seemed to be scolding, the noise made when a stranger comes into the wrong territory or too close to a nest. Teresa tried to speak to the raven but had no success until, at last, the animal seemed to get hold of herself and calm down.

What are you doing? the bird asked. Why are these people still here? Why are you dilly-dallying?

Teresa was startled and then irritated. Who are *you*? she snapped back, meaning who are *you* to scold or tell me what to do?

The raven gave a hop, hop, next to the sleeping boy. Who am I? You should know. You've been looking for me. You've been calling out my name.

I haven't, Teresa protested even as she tried to think back. Ravens had come to her all her life, of course, for they were naturally curious and common birds, always interested in what humans were doing. A raven had stared down at her from a scraggly pine the day her father met with the Spanish slavers, their armor glinting in the sun. And there had been ravens, as well, by the kitchen door of the Governor's house and in the garden and in the stables and at all the places where the villagers threw their waste. On her journey with Horse and Pomo, ravens had cried and swooshed trying to drive her away from a prickly pear patch or jojoba bush. Ravens had come to her more than once, but she had never gone looking for them. She had never called out to them.

The bird gurgle-croaked. You really don't recognize me?

I really don't, Teresa said.

At this, the raven lifted one yellow foot and balanced improbably, foot raised. Go on. Take a look.

Teresa hesitated.

The raven hopped and hissed. I can't do this all day!

Reluctantly, Teresa bent close, thinking that she was no longer a servant in the Governor's house. She no longer had to do whatever an assistant to an assistant cook told her to do.

On the raven's upraised talon, a short white line slashed the yellow skin. A scar angled there like a scar on the palm of a human hand. Teresa felt a tickling at the back of her mind, tickling like a feather.

The colors were so beautiful, the raven said, gold-green, the fins red, the back scalloped and edged with orange. I was young and wanted to take my prize home.

You threw the fish into the grass with a scream! Teresa remembered.

The raven cawed.

You're the girl with long black hair swimming through fire. Like wind moves through the branches of a tree. Teresa had said those words so often, to Pomo, to herself.

The raven preened. I was. I am.

You burned your hand. You're a shape-shifter. Again Teresa felt that tickle.

The raven continued the story Teresa had first heard when she was small.

After that day—the raven gave another *tlok-tlok-tlok*—I didn't go back into the earth for a long time. You can't just go back and forth. You won't have the strength. And you can't stay here much longer, or you will never go back. That's why you need to take these hunters to their village. You need to take the boy. Give him a good bath!

Teresa glanced, embarrassed, at Pomo. The boy looked fine—maybe just a little dirty. Maybe his hair did need combing.

What are you waiting for? the raven asked, but it was not a real question. *Krooo-ak!* the bird screeched.

Tlok-tlok-tlok.

And suddenly, Teresa made the same gesture she had made with the Opata hunters, flapping her arms. Shoo! Shoo! she waved her hands. It was what they did when turkeys and chickens got too close to the kitchen door. Go away, Teresa shouted. I no longer jump when someone gives an order!

Not even for you, Teresa thought, not even for the girl with long black hair.

The surprised raven fell back, cawed, and flapped her wings. You know what you saw, the raven called down, circling upward, growing smaller. You know what really happened.

Brushstrokes in the air. Feathers and fire. The memory of that fever burned Teresa again. The memory of those chills swept through her body. She had seen wonderful things. She had seen the wise woman, the seashell necklace with gleams of coral pink. The wise woman spoke. The wise woman was Plague clouding her thoughts. Plague had tricked her.

But not only Plague—before then, too. Before Plague, long before, she had tricked herself. She had deliberately forgotten. Buried deep. In the coolness of the adobe house, the wise woman had raised her hand. She had lifted her palm so that Teresa could see the scar from the gold-green, red-orange fish that once burned her. The wise woman had looked straight at her father, but she had held up her hand for Teresa to see. The black-haired girl was the wise woman was a shape-shifter was the raven. Teresa had stared back, the songs of the hill still running in her veins, the coyote pup and the music of flowers. Then she had gone to lean against her father's leg, her father who was so pleased to have found the Spanish helmet.

You made your choice, the earth said. You loved your father. You were only a child.

Come back, come back, Teresa yelled up to the sky of stone.

She won't come back now, the earth predicted. You've insulted her.

The black speck reappeared and landed close by.

So now you do want me, the raven sounded petulant.

Plague said you were dead! You had the *sarampión*!

The bird cocked her head as ravens do, as if trying to see something more clearly. And so you believed him—that trickster? Well, yes, I had the *sarampión*. He told the truth about that. I was dying, a hair away, and I would have died if I had not shifted into being a raven. I will die if I shift back to human form. How old are you?

The question was so abrupt. Teresa had to think and count on her fingers. What had happened when?

The raven continued to talk, as if to herself: it's never good to be too long an animal. When I started to like the taste of carrion, when I spent whole days searching for grubs, I went into the earth. I knew I could stay myself here.

Teresa had her answer. Sixteen? she guessed.

Black wings fluttered and the raven gaped, opening and reopening her beak. That long? the bird squawked. And then sharply: are you ready? It is past time.

And Teresa knew the wise woman was right. She had to choose again—where to go, who she would be—and, of course, she chose Pomo. She would give him his life and return to her own.

You're leaving me, the earth said sadly.

The world is changing, Teresa replied in the same sad tone, and then shrugged as if to admit she was part of that change.

You won't come back soon, the earth said. You won't have the strength.

Take the hunters first, the raven suggested. I'll stay with the boy.

Teresa arrowed up to the hot desert floor, the limp body of a hunter dangling from each hand, their weight not much more to her than two rabbits. She flew through fields of volcanic rock and beds of limestone. She flew through crystals, the tingle of quartz and feldspar. Briefly she followed a vein of copper with its musical hum. Briefly she passed through a richer ore, softer and more lustrous, the power of gold. Above all things, Andrés Dorantes, Alonso del Castillo, and Cabeza de Vaca had loved gold. They had dreamed of gold that lined the streets of Indian villages, rooms filled with gold bars and gold masks and gold jewelry like Hernán Cortés had seen in the treasure vaults of the great Montezuma. They had talked of the gold they had seen themselves when they were young, in Spanish homes and Spanish palaces, for they had heard this song all their lives. Even Teresa was intrigued by the metal's promises.

But she didn't pause. She flew up and then angled to where the earthquake had thrown the Opatas to the ground and Horse had run away. From here, the two men were less than a day from their village in the thorn forest on the edge of the desert. Plague would not bother them since they no longer carried the gift of *sarampión*. The Opatas would stumble back to their families, who would surely wonder where they had been and what they had been doing these last few weeks.

The men would answer, Teresa thought, by shaking their heads and looking at the ground. They would touch the scars on their skin. They would remember the Opata elder from a far-off village and the horse and the boy and the ugly witch with an ugly flattened head and ugly tattoos. They would be bewildered by a jumble of strange images. They would not know what to tell their wives and children.

When Teresa reached the right place, she heaved the hunters up and out, one by one, so that they cleared the ground and landed roughly. She did not care about being gentle. These men had left Pomo unprotected in the sun to die. She had not forgotten that. Oh, Plague was convincing, Teresa knew. Plague had told them this was for the best. They had no choice. It was the witch who had really killed the boy. Plague was cunning. He had commanded, and they had obeyed. Still, she let the hunters land in a tumble: a few bruises did not trouble her.

The men's clothes and water bags lay where they had been stripped off so rapidly before. Teresa waited for the hunters to stir and open their eyes, which they did soon after they were on solid ground, breathing fresh air under a blue sky. It took them minutes more to be fully awake, and Teresa waited for that, too, because she wanted to see them stare with horror at the figure of a girl half-rising from the earth and half-caught in the earth, a girl with four blue marks on each cheek. With difficulty, the hunters scrabbled away as if their legs and arms were not working properly. One of them whimpered. Eventually, Teresa knew, they would be begging for mercy. She nodded, satisfied.

She went back for Pomo.

The raven waited by the sleeping boy. Without further discussion, as if the matter had already been decided, the bird flapped her wings and gathered lift for flight. I'm going with you, the bird declared.

Teresa thought of what the wise woman had said: you couldn't stay too long as an animal. She remembered how Pomo had disappeared inside the jaguar. Yet the raven couldn't shift back to being the wise woman dying of *sarampión*.

But if you leave the earth, Teresa asked, how will you stay human?

I have you to help me now, the raven called from above, flying faster so that Teresa knew she would have to hurry to catch up. So that she had to grab Pomo's hand, without thinking or dilly-dallying a moment longer, following the girl with long black hair, following the wise woman through layers of whispering limestone and sandstone, through the songs of copper and enchantments of gold.

21

The raven led the way along the path Teresa had already made in the earth. First they passed under the spring where Teresa had left her leather skirt, sandals, half-chipped cutting tool, and hard heart. They glided below the place where she had taken and then returned the two Opata hunters, gone now along with the cotton shirt Pomo had been wearing and the tinderbox knitted inside. Soon they were passing under the Opata village, where Teresa could hear footsteps, the pulse of hearts beating through bare feet.

Past the village, she listened for horse hooves although she had little hope of ever seeing Horse again. By now, without Plague to control him, he could be anywhere—west to the sea or east to the mountains or even back across the desert to his master's house.

On and on they flew through the earth, under the thorn forest. Teresa listened and heard at last the sound of water, small tumbling streams, water rushing over pebbles and stone. The rainy season had started. The thin-leafed thorn bushes were green and growing, and soon the forest would be full of food, the tall cactus with red and yellow fruit like that of the prickly pear, the dark mulberries and crunchy mesquite beans, the roots of nut-grass and agave, herbs for flavoring, and ocotillo flowers for a sweet tea. Teresa's mouth began to remember. Yes, it would be good to eat again.

On and on, following the raven, she held Pomo tightly against her chest. Teresa doubted now that she would have ever found the wise woman's house on her own. There was so much land, so many Opata villages, and rather more than one fang-toothed mountain.

At one point she called out—wait, stop. What if someone lives in your house now? The raven slowed just a bit, so they could talk.

No one would dare, the bird scoffed.

You said you got the *sarampión* soon after my father's visit, Teresa reminded the wise woman. A long time has passed.

The bird caw-cawed and gurgled in a way that was some-how reassuring. Perhaps, indeed, no one would dare.

On and on they flew, and Teresa did not tire—although she was perhaps just a little bored—until finally the raven slowed again. Finally they had reached the strangely alive, loudly talk-ing hill Teresa had once climbed to the wise woman's crum-bling adobe with its flat space for a garden and white bluffs falling to a view below. She had let the Moor and Dorantes and her father move ahead, gesturing as they walked. The plants here were nothing unusual, catclaw and prickly pear, humped cactus and tall cactus, yellow grass and white daisies, purple asters, orange poppies. But on this hill, they chimed like the bells her father had once given her grandfather. Even now, circling below, Teresa could hear them, could hear the animals thinking in their dens and burrows and tree holes, could feel the magic rippling. "Teresa!" her father had called from above. "Come on, precious girl. Stay in my sight."

Come on, the raven said and briefly stalled, flapping her wings hard and then flying straight up through the skin of the earth.

Once more Teresa followed, gathering her thoughts into a single force and breaking the surface, half-in, half-out, Pomo clutched to her chest.

As before, the world exploded in light. This time, though, Teresa propelled herself still upward so that her heels rested on the ground and her toes dug into dirt. For a brief moment, she stood straight, staring at a landscape of green-leafed trees and thorny bushes obscuring the edge of an adobe wall, a black hole for a door, a grass roof fallen in. The air smelled of rain and leaves, tannin from a scrub oak—with just a hint of yarrow, a touch of rosemary, a tang of wild mint. She had forgotten about smell! All those lovely odors!

Almost immediately then, her knees buckled, and she and Pomo fell, tilting sideways. Teresa's shoulder caught most of the blow while a terrible weight pressed down on her chest and every part of her body. She couldn't lift a finger. Even her teeth felt thick and big. Sprawled on the ground, she looked up helplessly at a gray thundercloud.

From the corner of her eye, Teresa could see the raven also knocked to the ground. Pomo whimpered and heaved and woke. Teresa opened her mouth slowly. The words came slowly, too, like the first heavy drops of rain.

The boy had trouble understanding Teresa's explanation. She couldn't blame him. He had been sick and feverish in the desert and now he was suddenly somewhere else. Now he was somewhere very different in the middle of the rainy season. With more ambition or strength than Teresa had, Pomo sat up and stretched and stared at the falling-down adobe house. He stared at the mesquite tree—where an owl once lived, Teresa remembered—and at the raven struggling to get on her feet, black feathers askew.

"Where are we? What's wrong with you?" he asked Teresa, who still lay in the dirt moving feebly. Like a beetle, she thought, overturned on its back. This was the weight of living in the world.

But Pomo was recovering much faster than she, perhaps because he had been asleep the entire time or perhaps because he was younger. Cautiously he stood and took a few steps and announced he was thirsty.

There's a spring behind the house, the raven said to Teresa. The bird's words were clear although she still lay on her side, beak gaping.

"There's a spring behind the house," Teresa repeated out loud.

"You have to come with me," Pomo said and squatted beside her, putting his brown hand on her hand, patting her shoulder in encouragement and then giving her fingers an impatient tug. Naturally he was afraid to go alone in this strange place. His cheekbones jutted prominently now in his thin face, and the skin under his eyes had darkened. Teresa sighed and began the painful process of reclaiming her arms and legs, first rolling up and over on all fours, and then standing with the boy's help. She tottered toward the back of the house feeling weak and a little nauseated.

The garden and field were a tangled mess, locust trees and cacti growing up amid bean plants and maize stalks that had seeded wild. Further toward the white bluffs, the spring trickled from a profusion of leafy herbs, mint and watercress, rosemary and yarrow, the water seeping cold and clear. A spring like this was a gift from the earth.

Teresa felt a pang. You won't come back soon, the earth had said, and she knew this was true. She had done extraordinary things. She had dragged grown men through veins of copper. She had swum through a monster with a gleaming eye. She had commanded, "Move!" and the rocks had moved. Now it was like a dream, quickly receding. Perhaps she would never be able to return.

Teresa put her hand on the wet mud near the spring and tried to listen. Silence but for the sound of water flowing. Silence but for the raindrops spattering—a storm in the air— and Pomo's voice in her ear, "I'm hungry." The rich-smelling earth was silent. She couldn't even hear the singing hill, the loud flowers and animals in their burrows. Coming back to her own life had drained her.

She regretted the loss of the tinderbox. There was nothing yet to eat in this neglected garden, although there would be roots in the thorn forest and some nuts from last year. Perhaps she could find a rabbit or lizard. But meat required fire, and she had never learned to use a fire stick.

She regretted the loss of her leather skirt and cotton shirt and yucca sandals. She was naked, and this bothered her. She remembered how her mother and aunts had gone naked, as had most of the tribes along that difficult mosquito-filled coast, and how her father had criticized them. Later in their journey, he had often mourned his own lack of clothes, for his skin peeled easily and the sores blistered worse on him than anyone else. Teresa understood these feelings better now than before. In the summer sun, her clothes had shielded her. In the coolness that followed a rain, they provided warmth. As well, they were useful for knotting up things, a handful of herbs or piece of obsidian.

Moreover, if she were to meet an Opata man or woman from the nearby village, she wouldn't feel as strong or as competent in her nakedness. This was something she had learned in the Governor's kitchen, from the housekeeper and Fray Tomás. Now she didn't want to unlearn it. She would rather have clothes.

"I'm hungry," Pomo said again.

Food and clothing and shelter from the rain. How much easier it had been living in the earth with nothing to do all day long! Teresa nodded at Pomo and went into the adobe house, looking for something to salvage there.

And how strange that the room looked much the same as it had so many years ago, with clay pots of all sizes lining the walls and bundles of dried herbs hanging from the ceiling. The air smelled dank, dim, and mysterious, despite the hole in the roof letting in light. Just as the wise woman had said, no one had dared enter her house or steal her things. Here was a knife on a low wooden table and a tinderbox on a wooden shelf, neither so nice as the ones Teresa had before. Here on the floor was even the leather skirt the wise woman had been wearing when she sickened and nearly died and shifted into a black raven. Teresa put on the skirt with a sense of relief. Now she looked more like the Opata women in the village.

But where was the jaguar skin she remembered? Turning around, Teresa saw Pomo holding it, his expression unreadable. Quickly she went and took the skin away, folding and putting it high on one of the shelves. She would deal with the skin later. Pomo said nothing but came to lean against her leg. She gave him a hug.

Oddly, Teresa was beginning to feel cheerful. Something about this house made her itch to get it clean. She yearned to find a broom and clear the cobwebs, scorpions, and spiders from the walls and ceiling. Then to sweep the floor. To count the clay pots. To gather firewood for the adobe oven outside. To fix the roof. To take down the old dried herbs and put up new fresh-smelling plants. Thyme and oregano for cooking. Lavender and balm for scent. To find some maize. To make tortillas!

She went to the front door. The wood of the frame had cracked and splintered so that the door was also cracked and fallen to the ground. Outside she could see the raven, upright now, wings still askew. The raven had been under the earth for so long. Teresa wondered when the shape-shifter would regain her strength to fly into the trees. Idly, she watched the bird stagger and hop. Hop, hop, hop. There was work for Teresa to do now, so much work, but still she stood at the front door as if she had a reason to be there, as if she were waiting for something to happen.

Here I am! Horse heralded, coming in at a gallop.

The animal shouted like a war steed, his mane waving, his nostrils open. You have been desolate in my absence, but now I am returned to the bosom of our companionship. Fair friend! We are reunited!

Pleased at the drama of his appearance and speech-making, the horse didn't notice the raven on the ground, or perhaps he only expected the bird to flap up as birds do at the last minute. Instead there was a *sqwaaak* and *kro-aack* and flutter and confusion around the horse's hooves. Oh, no! Teresa thought and ran to see. Horse was dancing back, and Pomo was suddenly in the middle of everything. Teresa shrieked at the boy to get out of the way and for Horse to be careful. No, no, she thought, but then the raven was hop-hop-hopping, gathering lift and half-flying, half-leaping to the nearby mesquite, where she clung to a branch with unsteady feet, shaking her head, and cawing furiously.

Everyone was angry now, Pomo because Teresa had yelled at him and the horse because his grand entrance was spoiled and the raven because she had almost been killed.

"You said you would get food!"

I've traveled leagues. This is my welcome?

Stupid beast of burden! Murderous Spanish cow!

Teresa felt like laughing but prudently did not. Horse had found them! How had he managed that? It was a miracle. And she had a knife now. She had a tinderbox. She would gather some prickly pear pads to bake, some watercress from the spring. She introduced the wise woman to the gelding— whom she was so happy to see! Slowly, gradually, everyone calmed down, although feathers were still ruffled, the raven occasionally bursting out in a *tlok-tlok* and Pomo eyeing the horse, remembering the bite on his arm and the way the big horse might suddenly push against him.

Teresa let the boy into her lap while she sat and Horse told his story, how the earthquake had frightened him more than anything had ever frightened him in his life, more than battle, more than Plague's wall of smoke. As the ground softened under his hooves, he had reared up and felt the release of Plague's grip on the rope. He had not seen Teresa rise from the earth, but he had heard her shout, "Run! Run!" and the next thing he knew he was galloping fast, very fast, until he could go no further. Only then did he stop to think and remember how Plague had confused him in the shape of his old master.

I went back for you, Horse said. I went back for the boy.

We were safe, Teresa assured him. We were gone by then.

The raven listened, too, and sometimes gurgled. Sometimes Teresa spoke out loud for Pomo to hear.

I had to find water, Horse continued. I returned across the desert to the spring. I stayed by your sandals, thinking you would return for them. Finally I came here as we had planned. I've been waiting nearby. I have pined for this moment.

As was his habit, the horse began to graze, nibbling the grass grown up by the house and neglected yard. Soon he would lose interest in talking. But Teresa wondered still how he had come to this place without directions or guide.

That was Plague, the horse said. He had to boast to someone, and he couldn't tell the Opatas. He was so proud of tricking you, of using the wise woman to make you come north. He remembered this old woman with great fondness. He spoke with unfettered glee of how he had brought her the gift of *sarampión* through a wandering Opata hunter. He exulted at how she had sickened and suffered, the inflamed sores, the bloody ears. As Plague talked on and on, I could see this very house, these mountains, this view. It was as though I had been here myself on the day she died.

Ridiculous, the raven said. He saw me shift. Such a liar.

Not you, Teresa told the horse.

I should hope not! Horse blew out air.

Plague is an old enemy, the raven mused, ignoring the Spanish war steed. He kills people. I heal them.

"I'm a healer, too," Teresa spoke out loud, surprising herself. "I took care of the other servants at the Governor's house."

Saying these words—the way they hung in the air, the way they took shape like something solid in the air—Teresa felt a stirring in her chest.

Am I a healer? she asked the raven.

Of course. The bird sounded impatient. She had not been a patient woman, either. Isn't that why you are here?

"I'm hungry," Pomo said for the third time, and the raven explained to Teresa that she shouldn't hunt the animals on this hill, for they spoke too loudly and their thoughts were too strong. The hill and the spring were a gift from the earth. Soon enough, the bird went on, they would be receiving presents of food from the village, rabbit and turkey and hindquarters of deer. Soon Teresa would be growing maize and beans in the garden, and they would have plenty to eat.

So, Teresa thought, that was one question answered—why she was here in this house near these Opata people. She would become their healer. She would learn from the wise woman, and she would learn the Opata language, and she would sweep the floor and make tortillas, too. She would put up fresh herbs for cooking and scent and also for fever and pain, for helping women give birth, for the stiffness of old age. She would look after Pomo and take care of Horse.

In her excitement, Teresa stood up, tumbling Pomo to the ground as she counted up what was answered now. Her mother and sister were dead. The earth had spoken to her again. Her father had loved her, and her father had left her. Her father was never coming back.

Then there were the questions not yet answered. Would she ever be able to return to the earth? Would Pomo learn to control the jaguar inside him? Would the boy grow up to be a responsible hard-working man? Would Plague come to this Opata village? And how would she protect herself without her hard heart? Would she marry someday? Would she have children?

Rain began to fall in earnest. The raven flapped and flew to the hole in the grass roof. Water was greening the thorn forest, water rushing to sea, a power, a magic rushing through everything, everyone and everything, each day bringing its own amazement.

The raven caw-cawed. The horse snorted. Teresa picked up the complaining Pomo and took him inside.